KU-125-691

JOHN NEWTON CHANCE

END OF AN IRON MAN

Complete and Unabridged

LINFORD
Leicester

First published in Great Britain in 1978 by
Robert Hale Limited
London

First Linford Edition
published 2002
by arrangement with
Robert Hale Limited
London

British Library CIP Data

Chance, John Newton, *1911 – 1983*
    End of an iron man.—Large print ed.—
Linford mystery library
    1. Detective and mystery stories
    2. Large type books
    I. Title
    823.9'14 [F]

ISBN 0–7089–9792–9

Published by
F. A. Thorpe (Publishing)
Anstey, Leicestershire

Set by Words & Graphics Ltd.
Anstey, Leicestershire
Printed and bound in Great Britain by
T. J. International Ltd., Padstow, Cornwall

This book is printed on acid-free paper

1

The first time I went to Iron House I thought I had run off the map. I had been on a quiet road running through a valley on the Herefordshire border and looking for a turning on my left. Suddenly I saw an overgrown track, rutted by vehicles, dive off and appear to plunge over the steep bank into the river.

Nailed to a great tree by the side of the track was a faded sign saying, 'Iron Ho — '. Unbelieving I went on another half mile, but there was no other turning on that side, so I came back and made the turn in onto the track.

I had been warned that Iron House was neglected, dilapidated, rotting away, but this approach looked too rotten even for that description. I was glad I had brought the firm's Range Rover, because, by the look of the entrance to the track, I might have to climb rocky valleys and ford streams through two miles of the Welsh foothills, for that was the distance from the road to Iron House.

The track went down, and instead of running into the rocky foaming river it swung hard right and crossed the water by an old stone bridge, the parapets long gone away, then snaked left and right between a forest of overgrown trees. Half of the trees were so furred up with ivy they looked like disguise posts for ten foot Martian infantry.

The air was dank, for the dullness of the day was made worse by the canopy of leaves overhead. On either side the slopes of the hills rose up and disappeared behind the roof of leaves. The rocks strewn about were bright green and brown with lichen and the black ground a mulch of years of fallen leaves.

The track rose in a winding course then suddenly levelled out in an avenue of trees with mountainous blackberry bushes, gorse and bracken crowding them on the left.

But on the right, over a field where a couple of horses grazed, I saw Iron House. From that view it hardly looked like a house at all. There was a blight of ivy on this place, not only on the trees but on the house.

It looked like a great, soft green loaf standing there amid the trees, with deep, frowning holes pushed back into the ivy to let the glowering windows peer out. It was a big house, of many windows and a great door, but all the rounded edges made by the ivy made it look small.

I stopped in wonder at the sight. Dilapidated, neglected, rotten as described. But with the millions of suckers the ivy must be putting into the stones and the joints there would come a time when nature would just pull the whole lot to pieces.

I stopped and looked at the map again to make sure this was the only house there; that this overgrown pile could really be the home of the fabulous Jerome Cardwell.

The map showed no other building for miles, just indicated the ruins of the old ironworks in a river valley a half mile from it. I sat for a moment and recalled my instructions.

Alan James, stockbroker, had brought his query to my firm two days ago and I was the only one of the three partners in the office. He was a quiet, bland sort of man, his eyes much sharper than the rest of him.

'You've heard of Jerome Cardwell, rich recluse, the Silent Man of the Foothills.' He didn't waste time, which was refreshing. 'For years past my firm has handled most of his transactions without seeing him.'

'Have you ever seen him?'

'No. I don't think he's been out of Iron House for thirty years. We saw his wife, she called occasionally, said what he wanted — which I suspect was what she wanted — and left.'

'Was she the only contact?'

'There were letters, of course. No phone calls, because he would never have the phone in case somebody rang him he didn't want to speak to.

'For years, as I say, we obeyed the instructions and advised where we thought best, and the account followed a normal pattern, except of course, for the size of the investments. They were always sound investments, big industrial stuff and of course, entirely British. He is an abnormal patriot.'

'Yet his wife was German?'

'Yes. She was the Baroness von Grune. Her first husband ran foul of Hitler and was shot. She came here and married Jerome just before the outbreak of war. And from then on she became almost lunatic in her patriotism for her adopted country.'

'So she agreed with his sort of use of his money?'

'Absolutely. Then three years ago she died, and since then the pattern has disappeared, and in a way so has the solidity of the investment. Sound blue chip funds have been changed and split up into a number of other investments to such an effect that it is getting difficult to trace what he does own, and the old capital is now much reduced by these manoeuvres.'

'He's dealing through other brokers?'

'Well, usually we know that sort of thing as you are well aware, but in this case the lost funds seem to have gone nowhere.'

'And that has an upsetting effect on the market, I suppose. Is that what's worrying you?'

'No, I'm wondering if he's still alive.'

'Well, what about his signatures?'

'Seem genuine. Of course, I realise you will say a query of that sort is a matter for the police. Well, I have a friend in Special Branch, and he said of course that there was nothing at all for the police to go on and told me to see you.

'In the meantime, he managed to get a cook into Iron House to find out for sure, and she reported the old man was still alive.'

'Special Branch put a cook in there? But it's out of their country.'

'He's a friend, and this woman helps them sometimes and is always glad to get a job like that, for which, I may say, we pay privately. It is important to us. It would be serious to be found handling a dead man's account as if he was still alive.'

'Aren't you satisfied with the cook's report?'

'We haven't heard for weeks from her.'

'She deals direct with you?'

'It's entirely between her and us. My friend merely made the arrangement to contact her. Recently it has become necessary for me to make certain urgent recommendations because of changes in the market. I have written, but the replies have been quite aimless. 'Things are best as they are', 'Sleeping dogs should lie' — that sort of thing, and unsigned except for a distorted initial that might be anything.'

'But he is very old, isn't he?'

'We're used to his handshakes. And the point is he has got a secretary there, a young woman capable of telling us what he wants us to do, or at least of telling us he's ill and can't decide.'

He got up suddenly.

'Well, Mr. Blake, I'll leave you to consider whether I am fussed about nothing, or whether you would wish to help. Here are some notes on the investments and the way they have changed and are constantly being changed further. You may think it shows some intention of disturbing the market altogether for some obscure reason. As you know, big investors so often start others following. Your opinion, at least, will be important to us.'

He went. I looked through the notes quickly, then rang the man I knew had put James on to me. He was at home off duty.

'I think you should poke a nose in, Jonathan. You like eccentrics. This is a hot one. He is an aged, aged man reverting to type at the last moment.

'I'll go back to before our time. Grandfather Cardwell founded the iron-works in the valley there, late 1700s. Made a small fortune but then the workmen saw bigger places opening up in the Midlands and went. Cardwell sent his money after them and founded factories all over the place. Built Iron House while the local works was still in action.

'Well, Grandpa worked like a beaver, father did the same, and because they did they piled up fortunes from building new works, investing in others, in fact, by keeping the pot boiling.

'Then little Jerry inherited the lot in 1930, when he was 25. Till then he had had his nose kept to the grindstone by Father, and when the pressure let up he sowed a few oats.

'Flash Sunday papers dug out details of his parties and labelled him Sex King and Ten-Girl Jerry. It seems he used to get up to ten girls and men, hire a hotel suite and hold very peculiar parties for two or three days at a time, then hop off back to work as if nothing had happened.

'Trudi stopped all that when she married him and locked him up in Iron House with her. They were both very active during the war running the organisations at full power, but it bust him healthwise, and at the end they sold up the manufacturing interests and retired to Iron House.

'She died a short while back, and before the grave gathered any moss he once more surrounded himself with lovely ladies. He's got a girl secretary, woman solicitor, woman accountant, woman housekeeper — all there in the bloody house, mate!'

'Who does the work or do they fight amid the muck?'

'There's a butler and valet combined, a handyman who does all the shopping and makes a quiet fortune in rake-offs, and a gardener.

'The nearest neighbour is a hill farmer who sells them stuff and is always hanging about for anything he can make on the side.'

'And there's a cook.'

'Ah, yes, there's a cook.'

'What was your interest that you made that recommendation?'

'Are you free tomorrow morning?'

'Yes.'

'I'd like a game of squash. I'm getting the flabs.'

'Come over. I'll book a court for half-ten.'

He came, we played, and afterwards we talked in my office.

'You don't think he's dead?'

'No. But what's his pattern? Being

10

bossed. When he inherited he followed all the edicts of his dead father, never changed an investment, followed exactly in the footprints.

'He met Trudi and at once submitted. She died, he remembered the escapades of his peculiar youth and liked some more women around him, so he got them — I think, for the pleasure of looking at them, mostly.

'But he's used to being bossed, and I'm sure he's settled down to it again.'

'Well, who got him these women, all apparently professionals? He got the secretary first, and she got the rest. The butler and handyman are indigenous, grew out of the ground there like the trees.'

'You think there's fraud going on?'

'I don't know what's going on, but there is one point which as yet I haven't mentioned.

'Trudi and Jerome were great patriots, fanatics, and they have over years been putting out protests about Socialism and the gradual degradation of the country. In fact, they have turned round to a sort of

Guy Fawkes' view that political parties ought to be blown up, and of course, someone who felt violently one way might feel as violently the other.'

'Creating another Fascisti?'

'Well, they are right wing.'

'But Fascists are only right on the Left. They are socialists.'

'Then he wouldn't wear that. No, I don't quite know what it is worming at the back of my mind. If I did, I'd send in one of mine, but the Department would want to know all about it first and they wouldn't agree to spend out on a hunch of mine.'

'Oh, I see. The catspaw — that's to be me?'

'You know I wouldn't do that to you, Jonathan. Not intentionally.'

'Just hopefully? All right. I'm interested because I'm interested in eccentrics as a personal amusement, so I'm sparing time for you. I'd like to see inside a recluse's castle, but here is a recluse guarded by a band of formidable women in glasses, cap and gown, so how do I get in and not be thrown out?'

'I have given that some thought,' he

said, kindly. 'It's for you to see if the thought's worth the risk you'll take.'

'Has anybody checked the women's professional status?'

'Yes. They are as they say they are, but what else, lord knows.'

'You want to know if this is a bed of spies?'

'No, I want to know it isn't one.'

'And you think it's cheaper to let the stockbrokers pay me to tell you?'

'Jonathan, I'm not thinking of spies. I'm thinking of more direct dangers to the community.'

'Oh, I see. So what you want is a sounding, not action?'

'That is it. You just go in on a business call that must take one overnight to get everything read and approved by the lawyer and the accountant. Just keep your eyes open while you're there.'

'They'll have their eyes open, too, if there is anything wrong.'

'Well, you're used to that, aren't you?'

★　★　★

They speak of lantern jaws but Philips, the butler had a face like a lantern, one of the ancient type with a candle burning in the middle. It was long, square at the edges and had a luminosity that shone out of his nose. His eyes were sunk in so far they looked like lost marbles.

I gave him my card. He did not even look at it.

'Ah, Mr Blake, sir, yes, you are expected there was a telegram and Miss Lewson, that is the secretary to the old gentleman, sir, will see you at once, if you will follow me.'

He never took any breath but poured it all out like a child repeating a lesson before it was forgotten.

The atmosphere of being an overgrown and neglected house stopped at the front door. Inside it was a fine old Georgian house, fairly well attended to, with black oak furniture, one or two iron decorations in the form of gong stands, letter racks and other pieces, with eighteenth century prints on the walls.

He took me to a door on the left and opened it, at the same time bawling out my name so that everyone in the house must have heard it.

A plump blonde girl of about twenty-five got up from behind a big desk and smiled rather like an animated china doll. I went in. The butler closed the door with a mighty crash as if he had misjudged the operation.

Miss Lewson asked me to sit down by the desk, which was piled with papers, almost as if to impress a newcomer with the amount of business going on.

So far, it did not seem like a carefully guarded castle hiding a wealthy recluse.

I sat down after she had and rested the brief case on my knee.

'I'm afraid this will take some time, Miss Lewson. Perhaps until tomorrow.'

'Don't worry,' she said. 'There isn't anywhere for miles. I'll arrange a room for you.' She had very cold blue eyes, just like a doll's. 'The brokers have made a query, I think.'

'Yes. My firm investigate suspected irregularities in investment patterns,' I said. 'There is a possibility that some person has had access to the brokers'

15

instruction and made alterations that could affect the value of Mr. Cardwell's holdings. It's important, you see, to have your confirmation of present investment lists and dates. It's rather a job, I'm afraid.'

'Oh, we can deal with it,' she said, and smiled. 'Someone down that end has been naughty, is it?'

'Well, it's hardly likely to be someone up this end, is it?' I laughed and so did she. 'The sort of thing we think might be happening is difficult for anyone who didn't know all the broking tricks.'

'And you'd want every item checked with your — list or ledger or what?'

I opened my case.

'Four files of photostats, I'm afraid.' I gave her the files.

'Well, Mr. Cardwell's investments are very widespread,' she said. 'I'll get Mrs. Fox on to these. She's the accountant. She lives here, so there's no problem. We also have Miss Harrison, the solicitor, but she is away until tomorrow.'

'Mr. Cardwell does not handle anything himself now?'

'Well, he is rather old, you know, and needs to rest a lot.' She got up. 'I'll see about a room for you, Mr. Blake. By the look of those files you might need it for more than one night.'

Iron House began to look less and less like some tycoon's Xanadu, guarded by troops and lions roaming in the grounds at night — hungry lions, naturally.

Except that, of course, I hadn't seen Cardwell, and it might be that I wouldn't be allowed to see him.

Miss Lewson came back.

'Mrs. Grant, the housekeeper will get everything ready for you. Have you an overnight bag? I'll get the man to fetch it. Is the car locked? No?' She went out again and came back in a minute. 'Mrs. Fox is coming down to see you.'

'Of course, you realise there is not a great deal I can tell her about these accounts. I am here really to get her opinion when she has been right through and compared them with her own.'

'Yes, of course. You are not an accountant, are you?'

The blue eyes were very clear and I felt

I would not fool the person behind them for very long.

'No. We are industrial consultants. We make enquiries into matters which affect the welfare of our industrial clients, and investment, of course, is their first consideration. Without investment, they go broke.'

'Oh, I see. Then you suspect that there has been some fiddling going on which affects firms on the one hand, and the integrity of the brokers on the other?'

'I don't suspect anything, Miss Lewson. I hope there is nothing wrong, that the discrepancies may be genuine errors, or computer blinks, but at the moment no such can be found, so we have to go back to the beginning.'

'And Mr. Cardwell is a very important investor.'

'The most important private investor.'

'Of course.'

The door opened. A tall, beautiful woman, dark-haired, with horn-rimmed glasses hanging by a neck chain on her ample bosom, came in smiling, as if quite sure of her welcome from me, which she got.

'Mr. Blake, how nice,' she said, and we shook hands.

'Mrs. Fox,' said the china doll, coldly.

'I've brought rather a lot of work for you, Mrs. Fox,' I said. 'I'm sorry, but it is most important.'

'Well, let me see,' she said and took one of the files as the secretary held it out to her. She flicked pages here and there. 'Ah yes. Yes, I see what you mean.' She flapped it shut. 'But that's what I'm here for.' She held out her hand for the rest, which she took, one by one.

We had filled the files pretty thoroughly from pages going back years in ledgers that were used even before the loose-leaf were accepted. I was sorry to give such a load of stodge to such a beautiful woman, but she smiled at me again.

'I must get my own books out,' she said. 'This is all rather a surprise, you know.'

For a nasty surprise, she took it very smoothly. She chatted for a while, then

19

took all four files and opened the door to go out.

'Don't forget dinner,' said Miss Lewson. 'It's royal command.'

'My dear Dolly,' said Mrs. Fox with another smile, 'how could I?'

'Of course you couldn't, Gertie,' said Dolly malevolently.

Mrs. Fox went out.

'It's very remote,' I said, looking out of the window at the overgrown garden. 'I suppose you have a well?'

'Oh yes. An electric ram, you know. The electric comes from a generator out in the stables. Makes a bit of a clatter, now, but Mr. Cardwell won't get a new one while the old one still works. He doesn't trust much that's new.'

'But then he's very old now, surely? Old people usually prefer old things, specially if they work.'

'Oh, he's old, yes, but the spirit is very willing. When I came here I thought he would be an old wrinkled heap in a wheelchair, wrapped in a shawl. Well, he was sitting in an armchair and when he asked me to hand him something from the table I had to turn my back and he pinched my bottom.'

'Oh, did he?' I laughed. 'What did you do?'

'I giggled, I'm afraid, and from that moment on we've had no real disagreements.'

'He's easy to get on with?'

'Don't look surprised. He's like anybody else, he's easy to get on with one day, impossible the next. He's not as old as his years. The Baroness — he always calls her that — the late Baroness, of course, made him do exercises every morning with her while she called out the orders like a sergeant major, one-two, left-right. Still does it. Four times round the grand piano, then once under it, up again and four more times round it again. Makes you dizzy to watch.

'Of course he staggers about now, and knocks his head under the piano and all that, and when he finishes he falls into our arms and gets made a fuss of.

'Of course he knows what he's paying for, and it isn't all paper work. He's very partial to a cuddle, and he's rich, so what?'

She laughed and I joined her though I was more puzzled than ever by these revelations.

With the removal of the restrictive Baroness and the gathering of lush ladies about him, he still hadn't left that gloomy place so far as we knew.

'I always heard of him as some crabby old recluse who wouldn't leave the place,' I said.

'Well, he won't leave the place,' she said. 'You're right about that. And he is a recluse so far as he won't have anybody in the place — no visitors. We have to keep them out, with Daffyd's help. He'll bounce anybody, specially journalists. He's the handyman.'

'Do you get many journalists?'

'After the Baroness died there were some. Now it's only a loner now and again trying to get a story.'

'The brokers told me to expect difficulty in getting in.'

'Not in a case of Mr. Cardwell's money,' she said, and her eyes gleamed with ironic amusement. 'You see, we are all interested in the welfare of his investments, Mrs. Fox, Miss Harrison and me.'

'I hope you're right,' I said. 'But isn't there any family?'

'None. It's one of those families which will die when he dies. He is the end of the line. But he is very much alive about his money. He wants to know every pound is alive and doing well somewhere — '

She stopped talking as she looked out of the window.

'Miss Harrison back,' she said. 'That's odd. We didn't expect her till tomorrow.'

I saw a woman walking through the garden towards the house. She was tall, big-bosomed — which seemed to be a required feature for Cardwell — long-legged and with a very graceful walk, as if she had been taught how to do it.

She was dark, and as I saw her she turned her head towards the house.

'She's very beautiful, don't you think?' said Miss Lewson, and I caught the hint of a sly glance directed at me.

'Very,' I said.

I could not go further and say, 'She always was; I knew her for a long time and appreciated her great qualities and gifts, only she wasn't a solicitor then, and all she had known of law was enough to help her get out of its hands and her name certainly wasn't Harrison, but nevertheless in spite of myself and what I'm here to do, I can't help but be delighted to see her again.'

2

The secretary turned back to the piles of papers on her desk.

'Well, that's Miss Harrison,' she said. 'I'll call Philips to show you your room. Dinner's at seven sharp. Don't be late or you'll get caned or stood in the corner.' She laughed. 'Mr. Cardwell is quite a small boy like that. If he doesn't get his own way.'

Philips came and conducted me out of the secretary's room. He fiddled with his cuff links endlessly and it occurred to me that they weren't attached to shirt sleeves but just sliding up and down on his bare arms. Certainly his hard shirt front looked as false as it was grubby and might pop out of his waistcoat any minute. He had a trick of looking into the distance and whistling sharply through his teeth at odd moments.

At the bottom of the stairs he stopped. 'Perhaps you would like to meet the staff, sir, first,' he said. 'Not that I think you are curious, but the staff are, and meeting them at the start gets over the problem of having them peer through the keyholes. The keyholes are rather large here, sir.'

I indicated I had no objection and we went through into a big kitchen about the size of a modern bungalow. The equipment there would have been adequate for a small, high class hotel. Obviously Jerome Cardwell was fond of his food, as his father before him.

There was a man sitting at a table peeling potatoes, and a commanding type of woman in a white coat standing by the main table and going through some items in a notebook. She looked up. She had brown hair worn in a topknot, gold earrings and brown eyes which looked luminous behind her heavy-framed spectacles.

'Mrs. Trellis, our housekeeper,' said Philips and stood back.

'Anything you want, Mr. Blake, just let me know,' said Mrs. Trellis and smiled as she added. 'We don't bother Mr.

Cardwell with anything about the house.'

I was aware Philips was watching me as she said that. It was a surprising thing to say, meaning so clearly that no matter what, don't tell Jerome Cardwell. Odd, in Cardwell's own house.

At that moment the potato peeler looked up and said, 'I'm Farne. I do everything.' Then he went on peeling.

'Where's Mrs. Lane?' asked Philips.

'Cook's in her room,' said Mrs. Trellis. 'David hasn't been over from the farm today. I expect him soon.'

Philips then showed me upstairs and into a room at the far end of the main corridor.

'I have unpacked for you, sir,' he said. 'I notice you have the telephone in your car sir. I think I should tell you, sir, that this is a very bad area for radio reception, perhaps due to the iron in the hills. The signal is very poor and interference too bad to be worth listening.'

'Thank you.'

'Thank you, sir.' He went out.

It was a fine room with heavy Georgian furniture and a four-poster bed. I went to try the mattress when my eye was caught by an oddity above.

The roof in a fourposter is usually open, but this one was closed by a large mirror looking down over the whole bed. The structure looked like a bargain lot from the bankrupt sale of a Parisian brothel, if any such places ever went bankrupt.

The view from the windows were all of the ivied trees of a wood stretching away to a valley. It was broken only by a lane which wound away through the trees in the direction of the valley.

As I stood looking out of the open leaf of a window I heard a shot. I knew from the sound it was a sporting gun, possibly a twelve bore, and thought someone was after a rabbit in the wood further down.

The echoes of the sharp noise running in the woods and the valley below gave it an eerie sound, like voices calling to each other over vast empty spaces.

I went round the room looking in drawers and cupboards to see what Philips had done with my things. The only stuff I'd brought was what anybody would bring, for after my briefing on the job I thought there was a possibility that everything of mine would be searched.

As I looked through the things then I saw no signs of search, which there usually is after an unscheduled poke-about.

I opened the last unexplored door, which I hoped, not too optimistically, might lead to a bathroom. Instead it was a luxurious, small lounge with decorations and statuettes so erotic I did not remember having seen anything so expensively and artistically sex-barmy in all my curious travels.

I closed the door and went to the window again to think what this reception was supposed to be about.

My visit was assumed to be that of a sober professional man discussing professional matters with Cardwell's professional advisers, yet here I had been shown into a room specially devised for somebody else's extremely private occupations.

As I wondered, there was a knock on the door, which then opened and a tall woman came in wearing a silk dressing gown. At first I thought she was one of the lush full-fronted assortment I had already met, but it was yet another, and not Miss Harrison, either.

She had long gold hair and as she turned to me she showed a funny face, not pretty, not ugly, but somewhere in between and very much alive.

'Mr. Blake,' she said, 'I'm cook, Jane Lane.' She brushed long strands of hair from her face. 'I hope you like what I cook. If anybody asks I'll say I was asking your special likes. We are very hospitable if anybody *does* get let in.'

'I should think so,' I said. 'Is this the usual guest room?'

She laughed.

'It is if we let anyone in,' she said. 'It was Jerome's room when the Baroness was alive. It was their honeymoon suite. Startled you, I supposed?' She looked towards the last door. 'Well, you're in for a few more shocks yet. You'd be surprised what millionaire hermits play about at. He's crazy as a coot, but funny as well.'

She came close and looked at me with a challenge.

'You know why I'm here?'

'Yes. But you've been a silent partner.'

'Because there's nothing to make a noise about, Mr. Blake,' she said. 'He's just a very old man going back to his childhood when he was surrounded by women with big busts who made a fuss of him. Now he's at the other end of life, rich and wants all that back again. Its psychological. All the girls are waiting for is his funeral and his money. No girl minds having her bottom patted if she can get fifty thousand pounds for it. I've joined. That's why I'm silent.'

'You are a very forthright person, Mrs. Lane.'

She came very close.

'I tell you what I miss after so long here, Mr. Blake,' she said and put her hands on my lapels, 'affection.'

I put my hands on hers. I wasn't at all sure what her game was.

'I'm sure you do, Mrs. Lane,' I said. 'It's a lonely place.'

'My husband won't be out for another

three years,' she said earnestly. 'Kiss me, Mr. Blake. I just want to feel like old times.'

As if someone waited on cue, a voice called from the edge of the wood below.

'Mr. Blake!'

Mrs. Lane backed smoothly away towards the door, as if used to such situations.

'I will see you, Mr. Blake,' she said.

I turned to the window. The housekeeper was standing down on the path looking up at my window.

'Has Philips put you in that room?'

'Yes.'

She frowned and it looked as if Philips was in for a rough time when she met him again. She was in command of the situation, however.

'Is it quite comfortable?' she said.

'Very.'

'Some parts of the house are rather — eccentric,' she said. 'So long as you don't mind. Philips had the wrong room, but if you're happy — ?'

'It's quite all right for me, Mrs. Trellis.'

She nodded and smiled rather tersely

then walked out of sight underneath, I guessed, to start looking for Philips.

And yet Mrs. Lane had said guests were sent in here. Was each playing on his own?

It was likely if Mrs. Lane had been right, that all the women were playing a game of waiting for Cardwell to die.

In which case each might be putting in some extra game for herself that the others did not know about, and thus gain herself an extra portion when the fatal day arrived; a game that incidentally involved making the others look unworthy in Cardwell's rheumy old eyes.

If that was the sort of playabout that was in progress at this place, I was wasting my time, but I hadn't seen Cardwell then.

One amusing thought was that of Philips quietly playing off one against the other then going off and chuckling to himself in some secret pantry.

I saw someone walking along the path towards the house. He kept passing behind trees and I could not make out what he looked like until he was quite close, and then I guessed this was the farmer, David, who till then had not been to the house.

He was dressed in an old jacket, tattered riding breeches, leggings and boots. He had a sack full of some knobbly articles in his left hand and a sporting gun under his right arm. He looked slowly from right to left about him as if ready, the instant he spotted game, to drop the sack, raise the gun and fire two rounds rapid.

He saw no targets and disappeared from sight beneath the ivy below. When he had gone I saw blood drips on the path where he had come, so I thought he had bagged something from the solitary shot I had heard.

Suddenly there was a great crashing and banging of a very large gong somewhere in the house. It was so violent it sounded like some sort of fire alarm. The din was accompanied by a shouting, but I could not make out what it was.

I opened the door to the corridor. The noise was coming from somewhere down at the other end, by the stairs, but the gong was so noisy I couldn't hear what the man was shouting.

Then Mrs. Lane appeared from a doorway one side of the corridor and fled across to the other side, her dressing gown flying wide open and showing her nakedness beneath.

A door slammed and the gong and shouting stopped.

* * *

I was about to close the door again when Miss Harrison appeared on my left. She was laughing silently as she looked at me.

'He just wants to discuss the evening menu with cook,' she said. 'Hallo, darling. Can I come in? It's legal business.'

'I'm sure,' I said, and stood back from her.

I closed the door then and turned and looked at her as she looked at me. Then we kissed for a while and I pushed her back a little.

'What are you doing here, Laura?'

'You'll never believe it, Johnnie, but I'm drilling an oil well.'

'I'll believe anything you say,' I said. 'I always did.'

'Why didn't you keep in touch?' she said, wistfully.

'You didn't want to go to quod, did you?'

'You'd have saved me, darling,' she said, and kissed me. 'Anyway, I had to go away. It was special business.'

'Like a quick crammer's course in law?'

'I know quite a lot of law, and I've got the books in my bedroom. Anything I want to know I just look it up. The jolly part is Jerome doesn't know any at all. If I want to get at something special, I just go into the town and see a solicitor friend of mine. He briefs me and there we are. It's easy if only you take the trouble.'

She spun away from me as if in some kind of dance, and sat on the bed.

'But why are you here, precious?' she said.

'I give you three guesses,' I said.

'Not hunting gold diggers?' she said naively.

'Or oil drillers,' I said, and sat beside her. 'Tell me, how are things?'

'Couldn't be better,' she said. 'I think I really will do well at last, and honestly, too. It's so nice to feel good and saintly.'

'Did the Lewson girl engage you?'

'No.' She looked at me with those beautiful violet eyes trying to magnetise me into swallowing anything. 'It's all rather odd, but I really don't know who actually did it.'

'Then who appointed you?'

'Oh, Cardwell. He appoints all the girls. He likes girls. He doesn't care if they know law or anything so long as they have shape, charm and a very wide sense of humour.'

'You are beating about the bush,' I said. 'How did this start?'

'I went to a solicitor about a cousin of mine who died, Ralph, my cousin, that is. He left me his money, which wasn't much because he'd been ill a long time and his partner had done him down and bolted — as it happened — right into jug. But they never recovered the money.

'Well, when I was young and honest I had worked in Ralph's office for a while and got to know my way about the simplicities of the business, before I decided it would be more profitable to use the law the other way about.'

'I know that part. Go on and take off the dear, sweet, suffering, sad expression, because you remember it doesn't work with me.'

'You didn't know I worked in a law office?'

'No.'

'It's true. I often lean back on it. Anyhow the solicitor I went to see was a man in Hereford. I spun a fanny about how much I had lost by Ralph's illness and death, and how I wanted to practice again, but couldn't because I hadn't gone on with my finals — I swotted my yarn all up before I went, don't you worry — and he was very sorry because I'm that sort of looking woman men like to feel sorry about, you know.'

'I have noticed that you are a sexy dame, if that's what you mean.'

'I gave up all that American chat.'

'Then don't spin another fanny. Then what?'

'Then he mentioned Cardwell was

looking for a lady solicitor with my measurements and that high legal qualifications were not important as I could come in and get advice or action if it was wanted.'

'He rode along with you on account of your lying charm. So you came here?'

'I came here. How sharp of you, dearest.'

'Wasn't the Lewson surprised when you turned up?'

'She got the impression Cardwell must have told the solicitors and they got me. Which is true.'

'Then how did the others get here? Fox, Trellis, Lane?'

I put Mrs. Lane in with the other two just to make it look innocently balanced, and to take a chance on seeing whether Laura did know about Mrs. Lane.

'Well, Mrs. Fox was one of dozens of women accountants Cardwell saw, and she fitted his requirements. One does need humour to get over the early stages with Jerome.'

'Is she qualified?'

'Yes, but resting, you might say, when

she picked up the Cardwell call. She had been with a big firm and walked out over some row with the General Manager.'

'But how was she contacted?'

'It was just on the grapevine, as far as I can make out. The professional grapevine, that is.'

'And Lane?'

'She was tipped off by somebody in the same way. And Trellis the same. There was never any advertising, as far as I can make out.'

'The attraction of Cardwell's legendary wealth drew you all?'

'Of course. As for advertising, that isn't necessary when you've got a very wealthy recluse, there's a great deal of talk about him going on all the time, and some of it has to be right.'

'And all of you are quite sure there is no heir?'

'That's been investigated for sixty years. He's the last of the dynasty.' She looked at the window. 'You know, I'll be sorry when the old devil does pop off. In one way and another the job's been the most peaceful, reflective, and yet funny time in my life.' She looked back at me. 'Of course, I've missed you, darling.'

'Of course, my sweet. Of course you have.'

She kissed me on the brow and got up.

'Ceremonial dinner tonight. I must dress up,' she said.

'But he only just discussed the menu with Mrs. Lane.'

She laughed.

'That was just to discuss how hot he wanted his coffee.'

She went out. It all seemed less and less like some kind of knitted-up plot to defraud the old gentleman, or hide some extremist organisation, determined to blow up all the synagogues and mosques in that country.

All that could be seen was that the rich man in his castle had organised whispers of what he had wanted and from the resulting audition of talent he had chosen these beautiful, happy hawkers of charm, which had made him happy and given them expectations of happiness ever after.

But then there was the other whisper which so interested Special Branch, that something evil was taking place here.

Instance, Mrs. Lane had reported at first, then turned over to silence, but there are two outstanding reasons why informers turn to silence.

One is overpayment by the opposition, the other is the threat of death from the same organisation.

Then where was the organisation? Philips? Farne? David, the farmer with the shotgun?

Impossible to be all three, it seemed to me.

But then there was Cardwell himself. He had lost the Teutonic drive of the Baroness, but he still had the money and the chauvinism to fly the Union Jack in the van of the bloody revolution.

But at his age, what could he hope to see in the future? But then martyrs die for no future.

There was also a difficulty about organisation; there had to be communication, and nobody came visiting. Could it be arranged by post? That would leave an easy and able witness in the postman, who would certainly notice if a bundle of circular letters were given or received.

Letters might be posted in the town by one of the lady staff, but replies had to go somewhere, and such a system of poste restante, even done privately, would not be instant enough for an organisation.

Secret societies meaning revolution of one sort or another, need instant warning in case of an emergency arising.

And then there was radio and Philips' remark about the bad reception. He would not have said that without it being true knowing I could go out and try it.

Which left the hill farmer and Farne, who did the shopping. Farne most likely bought a lot so that he didn't have to go into town very often, and also, by buying a lot, he got a bigger discount for his starving pocket.

The farmer, however, came every day, according to my information.

But there had been no trace of the usual literature on the Lewson desk. The papers there had just been a mess of stuff dragged out of files and drawers and plonked on the desk to impress the visitor. It had been old stuff, company reports, local accounts and that sort of thing, by the look of the files, going back years.

At the time it had given me the impression that Miss Lewson did little secretarial work, if any at all. The broker had complained that there was a secretary who might have done things to obviate Cardwell's scrawls and fatuous quotations, but who did not. The mess of papers on the desk had been shoved out in a hurry.

Laura, I believed, did little for whatever return she got. Laura had always been a great money-for-nothing girl, which is why she got on the wrong side of the legal fence so often.

Mrs. Fox, the accountant, might account, but the picture I had was that her main calculations were entirely on what there would be to come when Cardwell died.

The housekeeper obviously had to work to keep a house of this size and provide for the establishment of seven who, it seemed, had little entertainment other than eating.

Someone knocked on the door, and I called to come in. Farne came in carrying an open box of shoe brushes and cloths.

'Clean yer shoes,' he said, putting the box on a chair. 'Best do that. He'll look all over 'em, he will. Thinks yer souls in yer shoes, 'stead of on the bottoms.'

'There's a pair in that cupboard,' I said. 'Clean, I hope. Philips just unpacked them.'

'Everything gathers dirt,' said Farne, opening the cupboard. 'You can't be too careful.' He brought my shoes out and prepared to work after eyeing them all over to see if they merited his attention.

'Do you do the shopping?' I said.

'Anything you want?' he said sharply. 'I'll get it.'

'Not specially. When do you go in?'

'Fridays. I stocks up for the week, what cook wants, what housekeeper wants, what any other sod wants. Takes me all day.'

'Doesn't anybody go out from here?'

'Not much. They stay around case the old man calls. When he calls, they're expected to go. He's particular, but it's his money, innit? He can have what he likes with all that brass.'

'He's very old, too.'

He looked at me, thin and sharp of face.

'You wouldn't think so. Fact, I think somebody's going to be disappointed. He aint going to die.'

'How far is the town?'

'Across the field and out, eight mile. Rough going. Do it all right in yours. No roads before three mile. Goes through the old works ruins. Wagon tracks, some of it. Interesting, that part.'

He polished my clean shoes with meticulous care. I knew he had come with shoes as an excuse to talk, but so far, he hadn't said much on his own account.

He went on polishing with meticulous lack of need.

'What did you want to say?' I asked.

He started and looked round as if about to scratch his ear with the toe of the shoe.

'Me, sir? Say?'

'Yes, you, sir. If you polish that shoe

any more you'll get through to the second layer.'

He stood up stiffly.

'You have seen through me to the second layer, sir,' he said, then relaxed. 'Yes, I did come to sprout.'

'Carry on. I'm interested in old ironworks, old millionaires, anything. I find the place fascinating.'

He lowered his voice and leant forward.

'Don't stay too long, sir. That's it.'

'Why?'

He leant a bit closer.

'Because if you do, you might get your bloody head blown off.' He picked up his box, placed the shoes carefully on the chair and said, 'Everything all right, sir? Thank you.'

He marched out.

3

As my door closed behind Farne I felt sure he had not said all he had come to say. It's very well to whisper that a guest may be at danger by staying in a place too long, but there are all sorts of hoaxers, and Farne's warning needed something more.

A half minute later, I was proved right. There was a sharp knock at the door, then it opened and Farne appeared again.

'I left me brush behind, sir, I fear,' he said, and marched in, but closed the door behind him with a smart backward movement of his heel.

'There's no brush here,' I said. 'What did you forget?'

He stood stock still and looked at me. He was like a clockwork character, sharp in movement, then suddenly still as if waiting for someone to wind him up at the back.

'I was going to say, sir — ' he said,

having self-wound.

'About farmer David,' I said.

'Yes — ' The works stopped with a click. 'How the bloody hell did you know that? I never mentioned the man!'

'You said beware of getting my head blown off. Well, David always carries a gun, so I guessed you were talking about him.'

'He sells food to the housekeeper,' he said, clicking over his surprise. 'Food he grows. Food he kills.' He craned his neck forward and whispered in a hissing like a water jet, 'He's a slaughterman. Slaughters, cuts up, butchers, buries the bits — you know. Very inconvenient if he shouldn't happen to like somebody.'

'He would bury the bits, you mean?'

He stayed still with his mouth stretched over his teeth and his eyes like bloodshot marbles. He hissed. Had he not been so thin he could have been auditioning for the Fat Boy of Peckham.

'He is experienced, sir, in the hygenic disposal of offal and offcuts of flesh, also bones. He was a butcher. He kills lamb for us, also pigs. He also sells dog meat which he cooks in a big boiler big enough to get four people in.'

'Do you have bad dreams?' I said.

'Sleep like a log, sir. The secret being one gallon of home-made beer after supper. Guarantees the arms of Morphia, sir, you believe me.'

'I should think it might compete if not guarantee. Is there anything else you want to tell me?'

'I am giving you the wink, sir, to respect the situation, for otherwise there are the means of hygenic disposal.'

'But supposing anybody should come and ask where I was?'

'They'd say you left, because in fact sir, you would have left. You would be clobbered on the way out. That's the usual way.'

'Usual? People have been clobbered before?'

His clockwork stopped again. He had got too excited over his revelations.

'I don't know,' he said, suddenly. 'All I've seen is them go away. They didn't come back.'

'I thought you didn't have visitors?'

'We haves some. 'Bout two a year, but they have to *prove*.'

'Prove what?'

'They have to prove a serious reason for wanting to get in.'

'Who screens them? Who sees them to make sure?'

'Oh, Philips, then Miss Lewson, but we all listen and decide. It's our responsibility, see?'

'Why is it?'

'Because if we let anybody phoney inside, we all get the sack and cut out the will.'

'And you haven't been sacked yet, I see.'

'We haint taken many chances. They don't often come, true, but when they do — we're *on*.'

'Well, thanks. I'll make a note of it, but my stay depends on Mrs. Fox; on how long it takes her to go through the papers.'

'Great conks!' he said. 'Her? She'll take a month.'

'There you are. I must get changed.'

'I don't know what time dinner is,' he

said. 'We never do. It depends on when he feels like it. Regular old tester, he is. Don't you expect anything. It might be ten o'clock.'

He went out, having left a picture of how visitors who did get in were discouraged from staying on, and how, by never arranging times for anything, Cardwell kept his strings on everybody in the house.

Nobody wanted to be absent at the crucial time lest the Master be angry, and with a single stroke, deprive them of a hard-earned fortune.

To me it seemed that the staff both lowly and splendid were serving a kind of prison sentence and hoping that their cache would still be there when they got out.

I found it a little hard to take that the women I had seen could be so easily moulded into an old man's mischief by sheer greed.

I did not exactly believe that it was really working just like that. Woman is a gregarious animal, more so than the man, and being restricted with the other prisoners in the middle of a forgotten industrial dump made me think that such intelligent and talented women must be on to some byway of what appeared to be the main road to fortune.

With Farne's going, dead quiet descended on the house as far as I could hear. That was one more detail that added to the strangeness of the whole set-up.

In a house with all those people in it one usually hears noises of living going on, even if it is only somebody running water somewhere, but there there wasn't anything.

I realised there might be simple explanations for such a silence. The Master might choose before dinner for his siesta, in which case everybody would keep thoughtfully quiet.

To test the quietness, I thought I would try and find the bathroom. I took my things and went out. There was no mark on any door that I passed which might have indicated something different from the rest and I got to the stairs without trying any handles.

The housekeeper was just coming up

the stairs and smiled brightly when she saw me with my towel and small case.

'Oh, I'm sorry, Mr. Blake. Did no one show you? It's the next door to yours.'

Which spoilt my chances of having a wander round on my own.

'I'm sorry again,' she said, when I had thanked her, 'because there is no hot water. Mr. Cardwell sometimes turns his tap on and leaves it so that he can complain we haven't kept the boiler going properly.' She smiled again.

'Life must be difficult for you,' I said.

'Isn't it anywhere?' she said, 'for anybody?'

'Not by design, surely?'

'Oh!' She laughed. 'One gets used to that. It's like a naughty little one. You just go through the house afterwards, picking up the toys, you know.'

'I've heard of it,' I said. 'Well, thanks for showing me.'

'I'm not sure yet just what time dinner is,' she said. 'Mr. Cardwell is being singularly cantankerous. He always is if there's a stranger in the house. You'll hear the gong.'

She went back to the stairs. I opened the bathroom door. It had once been a bedroom and was spacious and fully equipped with the latest late Victorian plumbing fixtures.

The only out of place feature in the bathroom was Mrs. Fox, who was sitting on a bath stool, looking through a file and smoking a Turkish cigarette.

'Come in,' she said. 'Make yourself at home.'

'I didn't expect to find anyone in,' I said.

'I'm first in the queue for when the water gets hot,' she said. 'The old idiot has wasted what there was. They're brewing up again. It won't be long now.'

'What do we do then, share the bath?'

'Now there's an idea,' she said. 'After all, we are both professional people and it does save so much water.' She leant her head back and laughed. 'I tell you something: I can't make head or tail of these accounts you brought.'

I sat on the edge of the bath.

'Well, I don't understand accounts,' I

said. 'What's the matter with them?'

'They don't agree with much that we've got, but I must be honest here. I think the figures I took over are forty per cent boloney.'

'By which you mean some of the investments shown on your papers don't exist?'

'Well, if they do, I can't find them. Mark you, I'm not saying this lot is wrong. They may be right, but it's a toss up between the two sets, isn't it?'

She flipped a few pages and looked at them. I watched her.

'But you have checked your lists before?' I said.

'With what?' she said. 'The originals were here when I came and I had to assume they were correct. Any alterations in money movement have been made on the originals, and they don't agree with this lot in a lot of places.'

'Oh, you were handed complete papers when you started?'

'Naturally, I assumed they were correct, but according to your figures stocks were sold which were never there to sell.'

'Do you think you have been sold a pup?'

She smiled at me.

'It wouldn't be the first time. I have a kindly look in my eye — forgiving. Haven't you noticed?'

'Of course. But I was talking of gullibility. At the outset of a new job one must depend on correct information being given, and you didn't get it, you think?'

'Well — ' She flipped some pages again and thought for a few seconds. 'Yes, I suppose I do feel that, but only because of these files of yours. Till now I've been satisfied.'

'How long after the Baroness died did you take on?'

'About six months. Jerome waited a decent interval before stocking up with further females. Dolly Lewson was first and she acted as the screen for the rest of us. She's not a bad cow, really.' Then she added, 'I suppose.'

'What is the atmosphere in the household?' I said. 'It seems a bit self-igniting at first glance.'

'Oh, it's pretty good,' she said. 'You may think otherwise but all we overgrown girls took on the job because we each wanted to get away from it all. As men used to join the foreign legion — to forget.'

'Oh. You look on it as a sort of escape?'

'Well, it is. There's nothing whatever to worry about. There may be irritating ties now and again, but there are five of us to take turns, so the strain isn't too great.'

'And you don't get bored?'

She laughed.

'Oh no. There's nothing boring here, Mr. Blake. You may even pass the time putting bets on the odds of who will be murdered first.'

'Murdered?'

'Well, there are rows, you know. Big, wild, fire-worky rows and sooner or later, one must come to a conclusion.'

'So you do find tensions, even in this peaceful retreat?'

'Do you know, there is one strange property of peace that the longer you have it, the more time there is for tension to grow and want to get out. Regular wars are necessary.'

'And that is noticeable here?'

'We are civilised,' she said. 'We all recognise that tensions are building up all the time so we make an arrangement; this week I arrange to hit Phyllis, next week Phyllis can hit me.'

'But of course, in such an arrangement Phyllis might be really mad and hit too hard.'

'Yes, I see that.'

'Incidentally, there is no Phyllis here. She was the illustration.'

She appeared to be very cautious of libel or slander or perhaps just of giving a wrong impression.

But the impression I had already got from her was wrong enough.

★   ★   ★

Our conversation was interrupted by another outburst of gong-bashing. If anything, this was more furious than the first had been, but the shouting less demented in tone.

'That's me,' she said, getting up with the sigh. 'There goes my bath.' She went to the door then smiled and turned back. 'You may have my place.'

She went out. A minute later the gonging stopped abruptly.

It was a hell of a way to call one's experts into conference.

More astonishing was that when it happened, each woman knew who it was for, and went at once.

If that was the call of future money, then it was stranger than I had ever realised. Further, in my experience women thought only of money in what it could buy. There are few if any female misers.

In which case, what did the women want that could be so worth the waiting for? As Farne had hinted, the old man was strong and might last years.

That knowledge kept bringing me back to the thought that Cardwell was not meant to last for years.

In which case, somebody meant to adjust his termination.

But if that were the case, then all the

women in the house knew about it, and obviously, the men, if they weren't in, would have an ear to the ladies' keyhole.

And that could be a reason why it was wished that my visit should be short.

The idea of a rich recluse in a place where all visitors were discouraged, even pushed away, seemed an excellent place to organise a murder for profit.

The original skill of the women in getting in immediately after the death of the commanding baroness was not obvious to me at that time. I could guess, but one could guess anything in that place.

So far there had been innocent explanations of how the staff had been massed since the baroness' rule, and true, under the Newton law of equal and opposite reaction, Cardwell might have chosen a staff of mature beauties to ease his declining days.

But under the same law he hadn't reacted and burst out of his hermit's shell. All he had done was to get some inside to share with him.

The obedience of the women to the

gonging surprised, even startled me. An almost military style in answer to the call.

And that was one of the things I had been asked to find out about. A paramilitary organisation disruptive unit.

I had already decided that control of outside bodies from here was not practical without too many trails being laid to the existence of such a network.

To let imagination run free one could imagine the women having been recruited for strict training as political saboteurs under the experienced supervision of Jerome Cardwell — who hadn't been out of the house for thirty years.

It was absurd to think on such lines and easier by far to go back to the old and obvious idea that the staff had collected for what they could eventually get.

They could be almost unnaturally patient enough to wait for death to catch up on the old gentleman, but they might be able to do it as they had served quite some time already.

So far I had come across oddities, but they might have been expected from such a strange establishment.

The only sinister matter so far was presented by the accounts. From what Mrs. Fox had just said, the reason for the broker seeing me in the first place seemed to be the right one.

If so, who had fiddled or was fiddling the accounts in their favour? If Mrs. Fox, then she wouldn't have said as much to me.

The sensible way for her to have dealt with such a matter, knowing I was not qualified to supervise her checking, was to agree the accounts and let me go back with them after putting down just a few amendments to make it look as if everything was then in order.

But Mrs. Fox had been puzzled by the discrepancies which clearly she had not thought existed. I thought the gong had gone off conveniently for her to have time to think more about the puzzle presented to her.

It might even have been that the gong had not been for her.

It was so difficult, in a place of such insane complexity, to be sure of why anybody did anything. It needed much more acquaintance with them before I was likely to get even a good guess.

I washed briefly and went out into the passage again. On the landing Philips was leaning casually on the rail apparently looking down on something in the hall.

From his attitude it did not look as if dinner was imminent.

I went back into my room and smelt scent. So far that day I had had Mrs. Trellis and Laura in there, but neither seemed to have used the particular smell.

Looking round as I put my things down, I saw the door of the Odd Room was open.

'Anybody there?' I said.

Miss Lewson came out, smiling.

'Oh, I thought you were having a bath. Mrs. Fox said you were. Forgive me. Cardwell wanted some papers in a hurry and he said they were in here. I've looked and they're not. He banged all that gong for nothing. I don't think I'll go back too soon.'

'The gong just now?'

'That one. It's a system, you see, like morse code. So many bangs multiplied by a dozen. He's not an easy man to get on with.'

'So it appears.'

'I'm sorry to have bust in but when Cardwell orders you I've just got to bust. I hope you're not cross.'

'And if I were, would Cardwell excommunicate me?'

She cocked her head and looked at me.

'Well, he hasn't done it so far,' she said. 'In fact, he's been almost placid about you being here. I hope he's not building up to something.'

'What would happen if he was?'

'Oh dear! Let's just hope he won't.'

'He might get Farmer David to shoot me and cut me up for dog food.'

She looked up, blue eyes wide and startled.

'Good gracious! Why on earth did you say that?'

'Hill farmers are good at it. If there's one place I wouldn't dig up it would be round a hill farmer's house. Bodies galore. I read it in the Sunday papers.'

She laughed and looked relieved.

'Oh! I wondered what you meant. We

don't have papers here, just the Financial Times every Monday.'

'Every Monday? What about the rest of the week?'

'They don't matter. You see, it's only for the game.'

'Oh, dear, everything is so new round here. What game do you play with the Financial Times?'

'A sort of Monopoly, but we make it up ourselves. We all sit round a big table downstairs and buy shares and sell them — you know the game, do you?'

'Yes. But I don't know your version. How does that work?'

'Well, Jerome gives us credits of so many thousands, and then he puts out a board with all the shares and prices marked on them, and we buy and sell to see how much we can make from the deals.'

'Who prepares the board each day?'

'He does, of course. He gets the paper every Monday and works out what he thinks will happen to the shares during the week and each day alters the board to what he thinks.'

'So he actually controls the game?'

'Well, no, not exactly, because you see when we buy something, it alters the price, and if you sell, it alters the price again. You see.'

'But if you all combine to push the price up?'

'He sells his holdings and you're left with a dead duck.'

'I see. What sort of money is this you play for?'

'His sort of money. He credits us with it or debits, as if we have accounts with him.'

'And what if you go broke?'

'Oh.' She laughed. 'Then you get a beating.'

'What do you mean by that?'

'Six wallops on the bottom with a cane.'

I looked at her laughing.

'You're pulling my leg,' I said.

'My dear boy — I mean, Mr. Blake, I am not. We get the cane, just as at school, because he's got so old now he thinks about his young days all the time. The winner has to beat the loser, so it isn't that furious. It just amuses him. We all think he's imagined himself into being his old schoolmaster. But we don't often go bust. We are playing for real, in that sense.'

'I thought you said — '

'Credit? Ah, yes. But it is credit. We can draw on it if we need to very specially.'

'Money?'

'Of course. It's a gambling game, isn't it?'

'You said Monopoly, and therefore I was thinking of the little bank notes and so on.'

'No, no. This is money. Like in a bank account.'

So now I had another aspect of lunacy to consider. And lunacy of a kind that could make it worth while for somebody to take a chance of more than winning a gambling game.

But, on the other hand, the game was based on real figures at the start of each week, and the betting trends might teach somebody to fiddle real figures in the old man's investments.

'It sounds almost brilliant, as a game,' I

said. 'Who invented it?'

'Jerome and his wife, when she was alive — ' She laughed again, and added, ' — I hope.'

'Why? Do you have ghosts here?'

'You must be joking. This place is crawling with them. There are so many noises in the night if it gets too loud and you can't sleep you just shout through the door, 'Thank you, Henry, that's enough, dear', and it stops. You have to get used to ghosts, you know. Be friendly. That's the thing.'

'Why Henry?'

'Ghosts aren't particular about names, you know. Not a bit. Nor sexes either. They haven't got any, you see.'

'Well, thanks for the metaphysical information. I am surprised.'

'You are astonished,' she corrected, and settled herself more comfortably in the chair. 'Tell me — just me, I mean — why the hullaballoo which has suddenly arisen about Jerome's shares? Isn't there really any money left?'

'Of course there is money left. Lots of it. The problem is just where it all is.

Some of the records seem to be missing, that's all. Why? You wouldn't go if he was really broke, would you?'

'I'd have to think about it, if it ever came about, but it isn't likely to, I think.' She looked at me gravely. 'Mr. Blake, may I ask you a personal question?'

'Miss Lewson, you must know that it depends on what the question is.'

'Oh, I know that, and it will be answerable if you are honest.'

'Of course I am honest, Miss Lewson.' I smiled and sat on the edge of the bed. 'What is the question?'

'Do you like women?'

'Of course I do.'

'Then there is one thing you must be prepared for when you meet Jerome in a minute.'

'And that is?'

'He doesn't like women. You mustn't mention them. In short, there are no women here.'

4

'By that I suppose you mean that Mr. Cardwell is all for no sex discrimination?' I said.

'Exactly,' Miss Lewson said. 'He says there's no reason why the General shouldn't be a woman, so all are equal in this establishment.'

'A general?' I said. 'Does he think in military terms?'

'Well, what is there women aren't but generals, admirals and air marshals?'

'True. He's not proposing to revive the Amazons, is he?'

'Not with us, he isn't,' she said firmly. 'We are just office staff, not general staff. Besides, who would he fight? There's no war on.'

'He sounds as if he could start one.'

She laughed.

'Not him. He'd be the first one under the piano.'

It was growing dusk outside. The smell

of autumn from the woods was pleasant.

'What time do you think dinner will be?' I said.

'Well, usually, if there's a stranger about, it's nearly ten before he can brace himself to face them.'

'Bad as that is he? Shy?'

'Just peculiar, really.'

'I was wondering if there's time for me to stretch my legs. I'm in need of some exercise.'

'Oh, plenty of time for that, so long as he doesn't know you've gone. If he finds that out he'll call dinner at once and make it awkward for you when you get back and find it half over.'

'He seems to be forever playing games.'

'It's not really playing, but you'd better find out for yourself what it is.'

She went to the door and turned back. 'If you want to go, use the side door downstairs and walk that way — ' She pointed out of the window. 'His room doesn't look out that side.'

She went out. She did not seem to walk far along the corridor before her footsteps ceased. I opened the door. The passage was empty. I walked along to the stairs, then down into the hall. There was a passage corresponding to the one above leading from the hall and I went down it to a glass panelled door at the end. On the right of it the passage turned and went down towards the kitchens, the way, I assumed, the farmer had gone when he arrived.

As I went to open the glass door, Philips came out of the door down the kitchen passage and came towards me with the gait of a lame camel.

'Can I get you anything, sir?' he said.

'No, thanks, Philips. I'm going for a breath of fresh air. I won't be many minutes.'

'As you please, sir,' he said.

Somehow I knew from that and the manner of his obedience that he would go straight and tell Cardwell. I hesitated about going, then opened the door.

He watched while I went, then closed the door himself.

I went into the wood and along a path thick with dead and rotting leaves. It was very still. When I looked back at the house, smoke from three chimneys rose up in vertical trails each aloof from the others. Here and there a small creature scuttered away through the rustling dried leaves, then became still again to watch and listen.

The path began to dip into the valley and on the right an old track of rough stone blocks, heavily grown over, joined the path and swallowed it up.

I stopped to look down. I saw a wandering stream in the valley flowing past the black ruins of the old ironworks, set on a hard which was the floor of a great space spooned out of the hill. There was even a half-sunk and rotten barge still tied to the wharf, waiting for the cargo that never came.

The remains of an old tramway track could still be seen running in between the ruined buildings and then winding away into the hill below. Most of the rails were missing but the track could still be seen clearly.

The river made a rushing noise from higher upstream where it ran over rocks. From the old works downstream the water was good enough to take the barges until they joined the Severn.

I heard the sound of slow footfalls in the mulch of the wood, and turning to my right I saw an old man coming slowly up the hill, apparently from down on the hard. He had a thumbstick and was dressed in an old tattered jacket and trousers tied round the knees to keep the bottoms out of mud.

He looked at me, and that was all he did, for he turned away at an angle and went on his way up the hill towards the invisible house.

Such a character had not been listed in the information given to me about the place. He looked like The Old Man of the Mountain and might even be something like that; a dweller in the old, almost forgotten valley, living on rabbits, nuts, fungi and fish.

And if one wanted peace, that was not a bad way to get it.

I leaned against a tree, had a smoke and viewed the scene and my own thoughts. The scene was the better viewing. I could make very little sense of what I had seen happening up till then.

The only things that seemed clear were that Cardwell was a raving lunatic, and that having surrounded himself with the company he wanted, that company was now engaged in getting from him what they wanted.

I stamped out the cigarette and went back through the trees until I came upon the old man of the woods. He was on all fours peering into the bottom of a bush. As I came by he raised a knobbly finger for silence.

I stopped and watched the motionless figure.

'Damn!' he said. 'You startled him.'

I heard some little animal riffling away under the leaf layer. The old man got up slowly with the help of his thumbstick. He gestured he needed no hand from me.

Upright, he looked at me with a frown.

'Where have you come from?'

'The house,' I said. 'I'm here on business.'

'A lot of business you will do there,' he said and sniffed. 'The place is packed full of lunatics. That man Cardwell should have been shot at birth, before he could do any harm. How can you do business with a wretch like that? It's unthinkable. You could do more business with a rabbit.

'And I'd have had that one if you hadn't sent him off.'

He turned and walked steadily away almost in the direction he had come, his head moving sharply when he sensed what might be a rabbit moving.

It was getting dark but a moon would be rising then though it hadn't yet scaled the hills in the East. I saw the old man go in a slow curve that headed back towards the river valley, still searching for his supper.

As I drew nearer the house I heard the motor of the generator thumping away. Through the trees I saw a light or two winking from the house windows. I stopped again, unwilling to go back until I had thought things over.

The river surprised me, though I should have realised that people never built works where there could be no transport and the old transport was always water.

That waterway had once taken streams of barges, and from the look of it, could still take smaller boats. It meant that traffic was possible to and from the works site without it being seen until far off the estate, where the river broke out into less private ways.

I turned and walked to the left where the old man had gone. The track which the Land-Rover used for its once-a-week shopping was clear but seemed to run parallel to the valley line, so that the track I'd seen going down to the works must have a junction with this one further up the valley.

Looking from where I stood the back of the house was at right angles to me, and three or four lights shone from windows on the upper floor.

Nearer than the sound of the motor I heard a metallic shifting sound, regular, like a sort of beat.

I looked round amongst the trees but could not place it until something bright flashed from the reflection of a light from the house.

It was then almost dark, but fifty yards

or so away from me I saw a shadow moving in a rhythmic sort of way. For a second I could not make out what it was, and then I saw the cause.

A man was shovelling earth into a hole in the ground amongst the trees. He seemed to finish filling in, and then I saw him spread loose earth over the digging.

That done he began to stir leaves with his feet, rustling them over until the leaf carpet looked unbroken.

He finished, shouldered the spade and walked away, humming softly.

I thought he would go back to the house but he turned away from it and went away through the trees beside the valley in the direction — as I understood Farne's description — of the farm.

There was no point in going to see what sort of grave he had filled in, because I had no light with me and if I had it would have been foolish to have shone it while the man was still in the vicinity.

I went back to the house.

There was some sort of hullaballoo in progress. Bells rang, gongs clanged, whistles blew and in the midst of the din, someone was working an ancient Klaxon hooter which sounded like a mechanical cock being strangled.

As I walked towards the stairs Philips passed me going at the fastest spidery walk I'd ever seen.

'Oh dear, oh dear, damn and blast it all!' I heard him pant as he went by.

He was just like the White Rabbit hurrying to be late at wherever he was going. He disappeared to the left at the end of the corridor.

The din continued unabated. As I went into the hall I caught sight of figures hurrying in all directions, across the landing, across the hall, in and out of doors, as if there were more people in the house than I'd been told.

In fact they were the same lot, hurrying to and fro, fetching things, calling out, dropping things, slamming doors and running up and down the stairs.

I stopped at the corner of the stairs in case I was run over by some flying woman. In brief flashes, I saw Lewson, Laura, Trellis, Farne, the cook, and Mrs.

Fox fanning herself with a file as she hurried along.

Then like somebody switching off, the din ceased, and suddenly, no one was there but me.

Philips came on the scene first. He appeared walking down the stairs in stately fashion. At the bottom he turned to me.

'Dinner will be served in ten minutes, sir.'

'Thank you.'

I went up to my room along the deserted and strangely silent passage. There was no light my end and the only light was down over the stairs.

When I went into my room I felt for a switch and snapped it.

Nothing happened. Through the window I could just see the glow of the yellow moon rising beyond the hills and that was all I could make out but big blocks of shadow all round me.

I made out one shadow that moved and a firm figure pushed against me.

'I was just changing the lamp,' she said. It sounded like Mrs. Trellis.

★ ★ ★

'What happened?' I said. 'Did the noise bust the lamp?'

'No. I forgot it had to be changed. I'm so sorry, but I had no idea you'd be put in here, you see.'

She pushed her breast against my arm.

'Lights aren't often needed in this room,' she said. 'It's used mainly in the daytime. It's so silly. I should have brought a candle. Have you a match, Mr. Blake?'

'I have a lighter.'

I lit it for her and looked up at the ceiling with the flickering pale. There was no light fitting up there.

'Where is it?' I said.

'By the bed,' she said, turning towards that furniture.

We went to the bed and she fumbled with an old brass lamp standard from Victorian days which stood on the table there. Until then I had not noticed there was no other light in the place. In fact, in accordance with the tone of the house I thought we would be carrying candles.

82

'Where's the new lamp?' I said.

She smiled at me across the tiny flame.

'Do you know, I put it down, but I was so agitated to get it fixed I can't remember just where?' She looked round into the gloom. 'How silly. I've been put out today, you know. Mr. Jerome has been so very awkward.'

'Because of a visitor?'

'No. I believe it's something to do with his business affairs. They are so involved and he gets so very mad if things seem to go awry.'

She sat on the bed.

'Do sit down, Mr. Blake. I do so need a man to talk to.' She patted the bed beside her. 'Be near me, just for kindness. I have so missed my dear husband, rest his soul.'

She took my hand and gently pulled me down. It is so difficult not to obey such commands when one wishes to remain friendly for reasons of one's safety.

'He is dead? I'm sorry.'

She leant gently against me.

'It was such a tragedy,' she said, sadly. 'After it was over, I just had to get away from anything that reminded me, and that is why you see me here.'

'An accident, Mrs. Trellis?'

'Very much so, in a way,' she said. 'The judge decided that it was and instructed the jury to dismiss the charge of murder. After all, he was correct, I think Mr. Blake?'

'I would hardly know,' I said.

'Oh,' she settled against my side and took my hand again. 'My husband was a butcher, you see, and Miss Lumby was the cashier, and that was the cause of the trouble.

'I came home unexpectedly from seeing my friend, because he — that is, she had been called back suddenly and when I walked into our sitting room there they were — actually — I mean, actually — and on my sofa! Of course, I did the only thing that came into my head.

'I ran down and got this meat axe, just to frighten him of course. Well, when I ran in again with it I caught my foot in the rug just as he got up and I cut his head as I fell.'

And then I remembered just such a

case some three or four years ago, where, according to the wilder Sunday newspapers, she had not only cut her husband's head but cut it right off.

'I should never have used such a thing as that axe, but in my desperation, I thought the worse thing I got the more he'd be frightened when he saw it. Only he didn't actually see it.'

She sighed.

The lighter went out. It must have got overheated or used up the gas.

'Of course, I sacked Miss Lumby,' she added.

'I imagine so,' I said, more than ever convinced of the wisdom of the old man of the woods and his views of the inmates of the house.

Suddenly, while I glanced at the rising edge of the moon through the window, she flung her arms round my neck and practically pulled me on to her.

'Oh, Mr. Blake!' she gasped. 'You cannot know how desolate I am!'

She started kissing my face like some sort of animated sink cleaner.

'Mrs. Trellis!' I said trying to be quiet

and calming. 'You must — '

Mercifully, the door opened and another female form appeared, silhouetted against the light from the distant landing.

'What are you doing there, Jonathan? Not before dinner, surely?'

'Miss Harrison — ' I said, trying to disengage from Mrs. Trellis who seemed in the darkness to have developed the wily limbs of a human octopus.

'Send her away!' gasped Mrs. Trellis in wild agitation. 'She only wants you and I was here — '

Laura, who seemed able to see in the dark, came up and did something to Mrs. Trellis which caused the lady to let me go, then hiss, then explode in a massive physical attack on Laura. The rage was so wild, so instant that I saw in that dark moment how Mr. Trellis's head had parted from him.

Laura, however, had had experience, as I well knew, and she had Mrs. Trellis's back up against her and Mrs. Trellis's arm held firmly and painfully behind her so that the virago was suddenly stilled.

'Now go and behave,' said Laura, letting her free.

Mrs. Trellis smoothed her white coat, drew herself up with monumental dignity and calm.

'Dinner should be ready in about ten minutes,' she said, and went out, tidying her hair-do as she went.

'Don't shut the door,' I said to Laura. 'There's no damn light in here.'

'You must be smothered in Red Paint Number 14 'For the Girl who wants a Date'.'

'I'm all right. Just tell me, is this dinner really going to happen in ten minutes?'

'Shouldn't think so.'

'Then why does everybody go round saying it will be?'

'They like to make you happy. After all, they don't say which ten minutes, do they?'

'What was all the shouting and banging about just now?'

'Project Exterminate.'

'What?'

'Jerome has a lot of valuable furniture, and is frightened of woodworm,' she said.

'Yes?' I said. 'What's that to do with all that uproar?'

'On the word of command, we all rush about the house, shouting and banging and ringing bells, you see.'

'No, I'm afraid I don't.'

'You're really not with this place at all, are you, dearest?'

'Well, go on.'

'We go about for five minutes scaring out the woodworm.'

'For heaven's sake!'

'He got the idea from scarecrows and strips of tinkle paper they hang up to scare off birds. So he reckons the same will work for woodworm. The beetles fly, you know, so Jerome reckons if you can scare one flier off with noise and sudden activity, that goes for them all.'

'This gets worse, Laura,' I said. 'And how does he start off these extermination exercises?'

'He has the alarm signal.'

'That Klaxon, do you mean?'

'That's it. When you hear that you start running, jumping and standing still, making as much din as you can raise.

You'd never believe, but it's marvellous for the nerves.'

'I would believe it. I don't think, from what I remember, your nerves need any treatment, but your sense of caution does.'

'What have I done?'

'You called me Jonathan in front of Mrs. Trellis.'

'Oh damn! I didn't think.'

'She'll remember it and wonder.'

'I'll say we met professionally years ago, over a law case.'

'She may wonder why you didn't say anything before today.'

'I'll just say I'm keeping you to myself.'

'How nice of you, Laura. With the state of starvation your colleagues seem to have reached that should be popular. So far I have been approached by the cook, the housekeeper, the secretary and I'm just waiting for Mrs. Fox to come in with her figures for examination.'

Laura started to laugh.

'But you don't understand. This is Freedom Hall,' she said. 'We do as we like until the gong goes. You probably think

89

that would be like an open prison, but it is really most relaxing.'

'Tell me, when did you last discuss a point of law with Jerome Cardwell?'

'Oh, only the other day. A small point. I had only to look up the books.'

'Who's the old man in the woods?'

'You do switch about, don't you?'

'Do you know him? A ragged old lot. Looking for rabbits when I saw him.'

'It's like this. I have heard of him, but never seen him. As a hermit, he's degrees worse than Cardwell. If anyone comes near he just melts into the scenery. I reckon that's why he wears those clothes, camouflage. Like a chameleon.'

'He lives in the woods?'

'Well, Farmer David and Farne, nosing round have seen signs of someone camping down in the valley in the old workmen's cottages. They're all ruined, but tramps can find shelter in almost anything.'

'He's not a tramp, is he?'

'No. He's more of a cave dweller, I suppose. Part of the wild life hereabouts, I'd say. We had one near home when I was little. Always wandering the woods with a black dog on a long rope. We never saw that dog off the rope.

'When I grew up and understood things more, I thought perhaps it was the dog who wanted to be on the rope and wouldn't let the old man undo it. After all, it made sure the dog had an evening meal, didn't it?'

'And talking of meals, I'm getting hungry. Go and tell this crackpot commando I want some dinner.'

She was surprised.

'You can't talk to him like that.'

'I can talk to anyone in the way I consider fits the occasion. I have been here five hours and not been offered even a glass of water. Get this bloody organisation working, Laura. I don't want to take back the impression that the old man's so mad he doesn't know what he's doing. The brokers might take more interest and demand an investigation. You know how awkward they can be if they think they are being used in some sort of fraud.'

'All that for a glass of water,' she said,

and turned to the door. 'I'll tell the old crackpot that dinner must be served or the police will come and serve it.'

'I wish you had the nerve,' I said.

'So do I,' she said. 'I'll get you a sandwich.'

She went after I'd told her to leave the door open. The drifted light from the landing was all I had until the moon struggled up past the hill tops.

I sat on the bed and looked at the glow of the doorway.

It was true that so far, three women had had unmistakeable starts at seducing me, and the picture with which I had been presented was that, in such circumstances of restriction, this outburst would be normal on seeing a male visitor for the first time in a year, two years, or even three.

Whoever worked that one didn't know women. Furthermore, women who stood to attention when the gong beat, or rushed about scaring woodworm beetles, weren't likely to burst their stays at the sight of the first visitor.

Crackpot, I realised the whole thing

was crackpot, if looked at in one way. But if seen from the other, that Jerome had descended into his second childhood and mistook it for his first, then it began to give a glow of a certain, very, very simple logic.

The great stories of the beautiful spy seducing the secrets out of the bold officer might still be tinkling in a mind renewed in adolescence.

Could he have sent the women to play up in such a manner? Could it be that he had had me let in and then proposed to use his feminine wiles arrayed against me to find out just why I had come?

If so, one sweet lady after another hurled into the bedroom like pingpong balls was about the maddest —

And there it stuck. The mad aren't that mad. In my experience they are logical. It is just that the reportedly sane don't agree their logic.

I looked out at the rising moon and went right back to the first thought I had had in the case.

Was Cardwell alive at all?

5

There was a knock at the door, though it was wide open, and the long skewey shadow of Philips showed against the panels.

'Dinner is served, sir, if you would follow me.'

He turned his back. I followed him out of the room and shut the door behind me. Not that closing it would ensure privacy, as up till then my room had been used much like a waiting room at Waterloo Station.

We went along the passage and down the stairs into the hall. There Philips stopped and solemnly consulted his pocket watch. That done he raised a hand and snapped the fingers as if summoning some servant, but no one appeared in answer.

Having achieved no result to the imperious gesture, Philips muttered something I did not catch and went into a room on the right of the hall and straight through that into a quite large dining room.

It was splendidly furnished in dark oak, silver candlesticks on the table and every piece on that table was silver. There was a lot of it, all gleaming yellowly in the candlelight of many candles. It gleamed yellowly because it did not look as if it had been cleaned recently.

The surprising thing about all this splendour was that only one place was laid, right at the far end of the long table. Philips went up there and pulled back the chair for me to sit down.

I sat, and before I could ask where everybody was, he started the finger-snapping again. This bringing no result he lost his temper, picked up a silver bell and rang it with a fury I feared might crack it.

'Come on, you slut!' he shouted.

As there was still no immediate result to this din, he bowed his head with great dignity.

'Excuse me, sir,' he said, gravely, then suddenly ran out of the room like an angry giraffe.

A minute later he returned at the usual, slow and dignified pace with the cook behind him. Inside the dining room he stood aside for her to pass.

She brought a great silver dish and cover which looked like a huge silver turtle. She put it down and smiled at me.

'Specially for you, Mr. Blake,' she said, and stood back.

Philips came forward, a serviette over his arm, and whisked off the cover with a splendid flourish.

In the middle of the great silver dish, set on a paper doily was a solitary round of sandwiches.

I said, 'Where are the others?'

The cook said, 'They dine later. Is that all right? It's cold lamb.'

'Thank you,' I said.

'Wine, sir?' said Philips, opening a great sideboard. He solemnly brought out a half pint bottle of Guinness and a silver tasting cup on a chain which he hung round his neck.

He then went through an entire pantomime. He opened the bottle, poured some into his cup, tasted solemnly, nodded and then drank it. He then poured the rest of the beer into a goblet, put it on a silver tray and solemnly carried it round to me.

The cook curtsied and went out. A second after she had gone and Philips turned to the sideboard, Farne appeared at the doorway, dived unobtrusively under the table and I heard him crawling towards me on all fours.

A moment later I felt his cloth polishing the walking dust off my shoes. That done he crawled away again and dived out of the doorway.

'Mr. Farne is very particular, sir,' Philips said, and backed into a discreet corner while I had my Guinness and sandwich.

I enjoyed it. I was very hungry indeed by then, having had nothing since breakfast. As I ate I wondered what on earth I should report when I got back.

A serious-minded broker, intent upon preserving his own and his client's proper interests, was not going to believe what was going on in this place.

And my friend at Special Branch

would probably think I had made it all up.

Yet this inspired lunacy, this consistent, unwavering stream of irrelevance and general insanity could be the best cover for something very serious.

The stranger would be so enthralled by the pantomime that any suspicion which had brought him there would be swamped out of him in a few hours.

The point was that not one of the inmates behaved normally. Even Laura had got what appeared to be an unreal outlook from her stay in this bin.

Just as I finished, there came the bellowing croak of the Klaxon from somewhere.

'Excuse me, sir!' Philips cried sharply, and rushed out, with the tasting cup clanking on its chain.

It sounded like orders for another woodworm patrol.

I decided to take what advantage I could of it and have a look round. There was a second door to the dining room, and when I opened it I saw it led into yet a third room, a drawing room of

mahogany and gilt-edged furniture, bro-
cades and a huge silk Chinese carpet.

There were a dozen candles burning
about the big room, revealing that
whatever silver was about had that same
yellow tint of the unpolished.

Going through that room I came into a
glass conservatory and by the look of the
panels against the moonlit sky, the weight
of ivy resting on the roof of it would soon
crack the lot.

From behind me the din of clanging,
banging and whistling was faint, like a
train passing away into the distance.

Apart from the garden door there was
another in the main wall at the end of the
glass room. I opened that and looked in.

There was no light, but the moon had
gathered some strength and I could see a
study with bookshelves lining the walls, a
desk, leather armchairs and by the
window on my left where the moonlight
was strongest, I recognised a radio
transmitter/receiver standing on a small
table.

It was very old. In fact, I think it had
come out of an old wartime aircraft.

There was a twelve volt car battery standing on the floor under the table.

Such a set, if still working as the battery suggested it was, could give communication over a few miles even in bad conditions.

It was the first sign I'd had of there being something in the organisation idea. But could a man of over eighty really carry out such work with any efficiency? It would be exceptional if he could, but then he was exceptional in more ways than one.

The banging and clanging was still going on, as if actual woodworm in flight had been discovered hopping from furniture to furniture in alarming numbers.

I noticed that it was louder in the study than it had been elsewhere in my unofficial tour of the rooms.

It did not seem to be approaching but rather the study was receiving it better than the other rooms I'd been through.

As I noticed this, it faded, and was then certainly drawing away from me.

The shape of an electric lantern

standing on an unlit corner of the big desk made me decide to go in and have a look round for as long as the distant uproar lasted.

The possibility was that for that length of time I might be free from the possibility of anybody else looking round and finding me.

When I got to the desk I could see that the light that was coming in through what I thought was the farthest window, was in fact a glass panelled door to the garden.

That door was open.

Though it was not cold that autumn it was not a time to leave doors open at night in a private room, particularly one used by a very old person.

I went to the desk to take up the lantern, then by the angle of sight that gave me, I was able to see into a big leather wing armchair that stood facing the open door at an angle and about six feet away from it.

A man was sitting in it, head slumped forward.

It was an old man, his ragged grey hair spikily untidy.

He did not seem to be moving at all even to breathe and the shock idea came back to me that Cardwell was dead, and this was the remains.

Leaving the lantern where it was I went round the desk and approached the wing chair.

At that moment the unholy din stopped.

I looked towards the door to the corridor but did not hear anyone coming, so went to the chair. As I got there I heard a sudden click which sounded to me like that of a gun being cocked not far from my left.

Having heard such things before I backed sharply into the darkness between the nearest window and the glass door. A heavy curtain was pulled to one side of the door and as I looked that way it seemed to move slightly against the moonlight.

There came the sound of footsteps hurrying along the corridor behind the door of the room. They passed and went away.

The curtain moved suddenly. The

runners hissed on the rail as the thick material was slid across the doorway. I heard someone move.

The curtain cut out the moonlight from the old man so that I could no longer see him.

I moved along the wall until I reached the edge of the door curtain. Everything was quiet as I lifted the curtain edge aside and looked behind.

Nothing was there. The curtain had been slid across to allow the intruder to slip quickly out into the garden.

I went to the edge of the doorway and peered out either way, but anyone could have been pressed in amongst the great thickness of ivy on each side of the door.

After listening for two or three minutes in the stillness I did not hear the rustle of a leaf and so was sure no one was there.

Once more I heard footsteps out in the corridor and I somehow knew they would come into the study this time. I moved aside behind the curtain a second before the handle rattled and I heard the door swish open brushing the thick carpet.

There was a click of an electric light

switch, but I saw no light at the bottom of the curtain.

A woman's voice spoke angrily.

'That bloody engine's gone again! Why doesn't that thing get done?'

The door slammed shut.

I waited a moment then very carefully slid the curtain back so that moonlight would shine towards the door.

The narrow slit of light shone first on the big wing chair.

The old man wasn't there.

★　★　★

I slid the curtain right back so that I had a clearer view of the situation round the chair. At first I thought he had toppled and fallen to the carpet, but I did not see how that could have happened without my hearing a thump.

The woman — I was trying to place the voice, but it could have been any one of the female squad excepting Laura. I knew her voice too well.

But that woman had had no time to come in, lift the man out of the chair, carry him out of the door and shut it.

I stepped out from behind the curtain and looked all round the room by the moonlight. I walked to the desk to pick up the lantern but when I snicked the switch nothing happened.

My investigation of the room then took place by moonlight and though large pieces of furniture threw heavy black shadows I missed no old man lying on the floor.

I heard more footsteps hurrying about the corridors and overhead and therefore slipped out of the window into the open air, first making sure that I had been right the first time, and that no man with a gun was waiting out there.

I moved away towards the wood and walked casually, so that any one of the peculiar staff seeing me might assume I was again taking the air, which might, to them, make me seem more peculiar than they.

As I did not want to be seen near the study I worked my way round through the trees towards the front of the house.

On my way I saw someone walking

towards me from the direction of the valley. I recognised the farmer, David, by his breeches and the gun sloping under his arm.

He came up.

'Evening, sir. Nice night.' He looked up amongst the trees.

We discussed the weather, the woods and the chances of a shot.

'I like your gun,' I said.

'You know guns?' he said.

'I shoot.'

'See that one,' he said, and handed the gun to me.

I examined it by the moonlight. It was broken of course and unloaded. I cocked it and the sound was the same I had heard. I fired nothing into the ground and handed it back.

'Lovely movement,' I said. 'And you know how to look after it.'

'Since a boy,' he said. 'You the guest?'

'Until tomorrow.' I went on to talk about game on the estate.

'Gone to pot,' he said. 'No keeper for years. I keep an eye on things, best I can, but it's a big estate, you know, and I have the farm. Just haven't time.'

'I met an old chap in the woods. Who's he? A cave dweller?'

'Oh, you saw that one, did you? I best bet you didn't get much out of him, now.'

He watched me, and it struck me then that it might be a relative of his, or someone he could be responsible for.

'He didn't like me. I startled a rabbit he was watching for supper.'

'Yes. That is him, all right. But I don't think 'twas for his supper. He talks to 'em. He's man of nature, and a natural man.'

By which I knew he meant a crazy man.

He pulled himself up.

'Well, I must see what they wants tomorrow. Good night to you.'

He went off towards the side of the house.

I had no doubt whatever that he had been the man behind that curtain and that he had cocked the gun in case of need.

In which case he was a cool customer indeed to meet me in the wood and offer me the gun to hear the sound again.

Or perhaps he had wanted to know if I did know guns.

He had come up so easily, so sure of himself. Almost as if to see if I did suspect him and then to laugh.

Almost as if he was master around these parts.

I wondered if his reaction would have been as assured if I had gone after him when he was burying in the grave.

I walked slowly on, wishing that I had had a better view of the old man in the wing chair than by slanting moonlight. I was thinking then of the old man of the woods, I suppose because he was so far the only truly old man I had seen.

A weird idea came to me that perhaps, in order to keep up the pretence that Cardwell was still alive when he wasn't, they might sometimes induce the man of the woods to come and show himself to strangers just for a moment or two.

Except that in my case, nobody knew I would get into the study and see anyone there.

Unless it was to be for the benefit of

anyone looking in from the garden through that open door.

Anyone such as Farmer David?

But surely he would know if the great Cardwell was alive or not. He was the sort who would make it his business to know everything about the place in case there might be some detail that he could turn to his pecuniary advantage.

I saw someone coming out from the main door of the house, walking towards me. It was Farne. He came up and stood to attention.

'Sir, you are summoned to the imperial presence.'

'Indeed?'

'The old sod's decided to have dinner,' he explained, still standing stiffly.

'Thank you. I'll come in.'

'It will be in the ballroom, sir, at the back of the 'ouse.'

'The ballroom?'

'There has to be a lot of room for the sporting events, sir,' he said.

'Sporting events?'

'Yes, sir. Competitions. Tossin' the Pudden, Balancing the Egg, Walkin' on the 'Ands, Pushin' the Pea with the nose, sir. It's very spectacular.'

'I should imagine it is,' I said.

'Straight through the 'All, right of the stairs, sir,' he said, then turned smartly and marched back to the door.

His precise military behaviour was new, perhaps put on for occasions when Cardwell was likely to see him.

Military again. More and more often now some suggestion of something being military occurred, yet still I thought that I was noticing the word military because of the suggestion made to me at the start of this operation.

I went into the hall. As I passed the door Farne leapt out from the side of it towards me.

'Excuse me, sir,' he said. He dropped to his knees and repolished my shoes.

I was not startled because I was getting used to this fanatic. He finished and stood sharply upright.

'Straight there, sir,' he said, and pointed to a pair of double doors under the landing floor.

The doors shone from the candlelight

in the hall. The electric generator seemed to have given up the ghost again, for there was no sign of any light but candles.

I heard voices as I opened one of the doors. The ladies were all there but the cook, who was obviously still busy.

Another table had been laid out in the middle of the floor, resplendent with unpolished silver, cut glass and bowls of wild flowers I thought some keen lady must have looked pretty hard for at that time of year, until I remembered the glass conservatory.

The women all turned as I went in. They were certainly a beautiful collection and for a moment I envied the old man his charming staff until I remembered all the troubles irresponsible women may bring.

They had glasses in their hands. My main interest, of course, was not in the women but in my first sight of Cardwell — if Cardwell turned up.

He hadn't then. There was only Laura, Mrs. Fox, Miss Lewson, and Mrs. Trellis being attended by Philips, still with the tasting cup slung round his neck.

He offered me a sherry, and I noticed he poured it on a table by the window. He poured two, in fact, drank one by tossing it back down his throat, then solemnly put the other on a silver tray and came across to me with it.

It was my night for fantasy, I thought, for, interested by the butler's eccentric behaviour I wondered if he, by any weird trick of this household, could actually be the apparently absent Cardwell.

'A penny for your thoughts, Mr. Blake,' said Laura warmly. 'You nearly smiled.'

'It was a passing thought,' I said, 'gone in a moment. Mr. Cardwell not coming down?'

'One never knows,' said Mrs. Fox and sighed. 'He has become so unreliable.'

'At times he becomes plain stupid,' said Miss Lewson.

'He does sulk,' said Mrs. Trellis, more cautiously. 'It comes over him all of a sudden and it is really unbearable. Like a rude child.'

'A rude child with lots and lots of money,' said Laura, smiling, 'which makes it all the less bearable.'

'What would happen if you suddenly found he hadn't got any? That he had been swindled out of everything?' I said and looked around.

'But how could he be?' asked Mrs. Fox, the accountant.

'It would legally be very difficult,' said Laura.

'Bloody impossible,' said Miss Lewson. 'We are here to see that no such thing happens. That is what he explained when he took us on. We are his defence.'

And, in law, I had known defence to cost so much that in the end the man who won the case lost all his money.

Mrs. Trellis looked at her watch.

'It's nearly eleven,' she said. 'Hadn't I better go and see if he's coming or not?'

'If he doesn't come soon I shall eat somebody,' said Miss Lewson.

'That would be a change,' said Mrs. Fox with a quiet smile.

'I will change you, dear, one of these days.'

'Don't start the batting till Jerome arrives,' said Laura. 'You know how he hates to miss anything.'

'I'm sure Mr. Blake isn't interested in our little squabbles,' said Mrs. Trellis with a smile.

'Oh, I love little squabbles,' I said. 'Where would family films and tv serials be without them?'

'I haven't seen tv for so long,' said Miss Lewson, sadly.

'It's much the same,' I said. 'Do you know the old man who wanders in the woods talking to rabbits?'

They had all heard of him. Nobody had seen him. The likeness to a chameleon came up again.

'He was probably one of those commandos with black faces in the war,' said Mrs. Trellis. 'I often think of them. I mean, they used to watch but nobody saw them because they knew just where to stand to not be seen.'

'Pity you don't,' said Miss Lewson.

I began to realise that Miss Lewson was the main stir-up element in this odd set-up. But then she had been the original member of the staff, according to legend, and it might have been that Jerome had selected her for this very purpose of stirring up trouble for his amusement.

But why were they doing it now, before he had appeared?

And again I thought, if he *can* appear.

That idea that he was dead was becoming an obsession almost, like seeing the constant fleeting resemblances to military customs.

'I'll go and fetch him,' said Miss Lewson. 'He might be shy again.'

'If anyone goes,' said Mrs. Fox slowly, 'it will be me.'

'I am the secretary,' said Miss Lewson coldly.

Farne came rushing in, breathless.

'She's gone!' he shouted.

'Who? Be precise, Mr. Farne!' bawled Philips, walking towards the startled Farne with the silver chain clanking.

'Cook's gone. Everything's boiling all over the ruddy place!'

'Calm yourself!' snapped Mrs. Trellis. 'Why are you so agitated?'

''Look,'' she shouts out, 'I've had enough of this, I have!' And she rushes out the back door.

'Then I hears David. He shouts, 'Back,

Mrs. Grobe, or I'll let you have the barrel!'

'Then she shouts something rude at him, and the bloody gun goes off bang! She's dead out there!'

6

Philips seemed to take command.

'I don't think we have a major dissipation on our hands, madam,' he said to Miss Lewson. 'I will investigate what seems to be a case of suspicion and hearsay.'

'But who's Mrs. Grobe?' I asked curiously.

'It sounds like a case of mis-hearing,' said Laura.

'I'll come with you, Philips,' said Mrs. Trellis.

Meanwhile Farne had been standing holding the door open and showing signs of nervous anxiety akin to intense depression. He shivered as he let the pair go by him, then followed and slammed the door.

'I suppose we should all go,' said Laura, with a glance at me. 'I mean, if there is a murder, then we might all be involved.'

'Farne's mad,' said Mrs. Fox, and laughed quietly.

'Not *that* mad,' said the secretary sharply. 'If he saw cook run out, then heard the shout and the shot, something must have happened.'

'Then let us all go,' said Mrs. Fox, looking sharply displeased. 'But I warn you, if there is a murder I'm not going to wade in the blood. There's nobody I know I'd miss.'

'You said that very well, too,' said Laura quietly. 'Then let's go. Come on, Mr. Blake. I should say you have a sharp eye, and besides, if the murderer has a gun we might need a good male shield.'

'That is sex discrimination,' I said.

'We aren't taking this seriously,' said the secretary.

'I don't believe it,' said Mrs. Fox. 'Farne's had another brainstorm.'

'Let's go and look,' said Laura finally.

We went out into the hall, round the stairs and along to the kitchen. Laura led the way, but I thought there must be a shorter way between the rooms, for instance, by going out through the french windows.

There had been a yell of murder, but nobody had rushed to see what had happened. It made me think that perhaps sudden cries of murder might be a part of life there, like the gong banging and woodworm hunts.

Cook was in the kitchen looking dishevelled, slightly muddied and talking fast, almost hysterically, to Philips. Farne was backed into a corner, apparently thinking that the safest place in the dreadful circumstances.

'Calm yourself, Jane!' snapped Philips. 'Who *has* been shot if it isn't you?'

'I don't know, and I'm not going out to see! I tell you I think he missed me and hit this Mrs. Grobe — '

'But he shouted out Mrs. Grobe, didn't he?' Laura interrupted.

'Yes, he did!'

'Then surely he didn't mean to hit you?'

'I didn't stay to find out. I was in such a scare I fell over in the mud. I was sure I'd be shot in the back!'

I watched but had no wish to make anything of my experience as far as murders went. I did not propose to ruin my careful industrial adviser act by behaving like a double agent from the Slobovian embassy.

I merely pointed out something that nobody seemed to be keen to notice.

'Has anybody seen any body yet?'

Philips cleared his throat and looked at me.

'Not yet, sir. I was ascertaining the facts first, sir.'

'Good heavens!' said Laura. 'The corpse will be decomposing by now.'

She went to the door.

'Bring a torch. The moon makes too many shadows.'

'Is anybody out here?' said Farne, trembling with excitement or something.

'I can't see anyone. Get a lamp!'

Farne went to a cupboard and started banging about.

'Come and give me moral courage, Mr. Blake,' said Laura.

I went to her. Mrs. Fox and the secretary had gathered into the interrogation of the cook, an exercise designed to save the partakers from seeing anything nasty without appearing as cowards.

Farne came up to us holding out a lantern which rattled with the shaking of his arm. I thought he was overdoing his alarm and despondency, and took the hard line.

'You go ahead and show us,' I said. 'And don't faint. If anyone did a murder out there he isn't likely to be there now.'

'He's had time enough to get himself to Aberysthwyth,' said Laura.

He came out into the moonlight with us, then fumbled the switch on the lamp and couldn't make it work. He did it, I thought, so that we should take it, and switch it on and then he could slip back into the house.

'Show us the direction,' I said.

He saw his fumbling had failed to impress. He switched on the lamp then led the way down the path dividing the big kitchen garden.

'Hold it,' said Laura.

Farne stopped.

'Let me remind you,' she went on. 'You said cook said she couldn't take any more, rushed out, then there was the shout at Mrs. Grobe and the shot. That right?'

'Yes.' He nodded.

'Then surely it didn't happen as far away from the door as this?' said Laura. She looked back at the house.

Her criminal mind was in full working order.

'I said I didn't see where it was,' he said. 'I'm just going by the noise for the direction.'

There were obvious questions which nobody had asked, and I still did not want to push myself as being experienced in asking obvious questions.

'What do you think, Mr. Blake?' said Laura.

'Well, he says the voice was clear and near to the door. Did he recognise the voice?'

'Shoutin' voices is not the same as ordinary,' said Farne. 'And there's the walls. Sort of echo. It was just a shout — high pitched, like excited. Well, I suppose you would be excited if you were going to shoot somebody.'

So even if he had recognised it, he was

not going to say so for fear of getting a bullet all for himself.

I looked around. It was going to be quite a search, even with moonlight and a torch, to look amongst all the rows of winter cabbages, spinach and other stuff, which all grew luxuriously.

'But where did Mrs. Grobe come from?' I asked Laura. 'Is it a mistake or a mishearing, or is there another woman in the house who doesn't show up like you and your colleagues.'

'I've never heard the name before,' she said. 'Have you, Farne?'

'It sounds a bit like something I bring to mind. Not Daffyd's woman, is it?'

'She doesn't come here,' said Laura, 'except to bring things when he's into market. That's once in a blue moon. He doesn't let her out much.'

'What's her name?' I put in.

'I think it's Roper or something,' said Farne vaguely.

'Could that have been the name that was shouted?'

'Oh no. It was Grobe. I wouldn't have forgotten that.'

I wondered if he was making it all up, but for the cook, who appeared in a state of distress when we had gone into the kitchen.

Another idea came into my evil mind and I looked upwards to the higher windows of the house peering out of their ivy wig.

The rearward looking part of the upper floor was, according to what I'd heard, Cardwell's domain. It did not seem beyond the bounds of possibility that someone had opened a window up there and fired out of it.

Up till then the invisible Cardwell had only manifested himself through his actions which, at the least, had been eccentric.

To extend his fun of gonging up wormwood hunts a shooting out of the window accompanied by shouts of 'Mrs. Grobe' seemed more like his work than a serious display by Daffyd, whom I thought would have said nothing but just shot, buried the result and walked away.

By that time, after only a few hours, I

could have thought almost anything about anybody, but particularly about Jerome Cardwell.

As we stood there in the odd light of that moon-swept garden I even had the thought that the baroness had not died at all, but was the actual gong-basher in the rooms above, summoning the lovely ladies as soon as they got too near her husband.

But would the formidable baroness have let any lovely ladies into the house at all? It was difficult to tell, for with screwballs it is hard to say which way they will break.

While pondering, we had a brief look along the avenues between the vegetables, but the bright penetrating beam of the lantern showed no body there.

'What do you think?' said Laura, turning to me.

'I think you should ask the cook what she really saw,' I said. 'She was upset, but why? What did she see to send her back in such a state, even granting she was at the end of her tether when she went out.'

'Ah, that would be theatricals. She's like that.'

Which was odd, and I made a special effort not to say so, for cook had been selected by an experienced officer to be the inside connection in that place.

Mrs. Lane had told me she had changed since she had come to that house, but I could not be sure about that, either.

Mrs. Lane might not be sure of me.

That is the trouble with this kind of work; everyone tries to convince the others he is not actually doing it.

Farne seemed to have become more confident now that he had seen nothing out there.

'I might have been too precipitated,' he said. 'But it sounded like blue murder.'

'I'm sure you were justified,' I said.

Laura turned and went back into the kitchen. I followed.

Cook was then sitting in a chair by the table, Philips walking up and down and the two women — from the way they turned when we came in — just waiting to hear what we had found.

Laura did not say anything and waved Farne to shut up. She turned to cook.

'What did you see happen out there?' she said.

'I saw this woman.'

'I thought you said you didn't see anyone.'

'I didn't see anybody but this woman. I mean I didn't see the murderer.'

'You didn't say that,' said Laura, amateurishly.

'I was in a state of shock,' said cook.

'You mean you didn't see anything there?' asked Mrs. Fox, looking relieved.

'I saw the woman! I just said I saw the woman!'

And in the midst of this harassed performance she glanced at me, and in that flash I saw she was really as cool as an icicle.

Then what had been the purpose of this screaming to-do?

I was getting tired, even impatient with all this idiotic scenario and began to wonder if it had been all organised and directed into making me so bloody mad I would give myself away.

It was as well, I thought, to keep that idea in mind. and my patience at hand.

At that very moment I caught sight of Philips' trousers as he turned to walk back down the other side of the table again.

They were stained in one long smudge on the right knee. Partly it was mud and partly, it looked like blood.

It brought to mind Farne's extraordinarily shaky hands, and the memory that sudden forced activity in tense circumstances can cause the muscles to shake about for a little while afterwards.

Cook was also dishevelled when I had come into the kitchen.

Now what could the three have been doing immediately after Farne had come into the supper room with his alarmist message?

Why hadn't the women all rushed out to see if there had been a murder?

And why had Mrs. Trellis been the only one to go out with the two men?

And where had Mrs. Trellis gone?

★ ★ ★

The sound of the gong and klaxon broke the uneasy quiet. Everybody responded as if eager to get away from the unpleasant atmosphere of the upset in the kitchen. In a second or two, I was alone there and the howling and banging of the woodworm hunt moved to and fro in the distance.

I went out into the kitchen garden and looked up to the hermit's windows. A leaf opened suddenly.

I ducked in at the kitchen doorway. A shot was fired. I saw a cabbage leaf burst and some earth fly up, then the window leaf banged shut above.

The banging and shouting was still so furious inside it might have covered any sound of a shot inside the house.

Yet there had been no uproar just before Farne had rushed in with news of a murder, and I had heard no shot from above then.

It is difficult to know what sort of sound to expect in such a large, solidly built house as that one, but the woodworm hunts could be heard all right.

I stood in the doorway considering the position. I felt sure then that somebody had been shot, perhaps killed, out in that garden, and that Farne's real purpose in coming into the supper-room had been to get help to shift the body and hide it.

If that had been the case then all the women were in it, for they had held back in the supper-room to give time for the hiding to take place.

But there was an objection to that.

Why hide a murder from me, when I wouldn't have gone out to look for one anyhow? I hadn't been in the kitchen garden before, why should I choose to go out there in the middle of the night?

We should have had supper and Farne and the others would have shifted the evidence at their leisure. Instead of which, Farne had rushed in and created a commotion, making sure I knew that something serious had happened.

Then suddenly, the klaxon had taken them all away leaving me to take a private look in the garden.

And at that signal the upper window opened and a shot was fired at me.

It was a difficult position for me then, for if I kicked up a fuss as a normal professional visitor should I would demand the police.

If I did nothing — and I certainly didn't want the police — then I would be suspect.

The reason I did not want the police was because it would bust the investigation into Cardwell's affairs open for all to see and effectively stop any success in the venture. Also a whisper that such an enquiry was going on might well upset the market altogether and ruin a lot of people, in the way of such things.

The row stopped. Cook came running back into the kitchen.

'Oh heavens, it will be late!' she said in an agitated tone. She did not speak to me but to herself, because she did not seem to see me.

For some reason, when I saw her turn to the stove and open the oven to look inside, I knew the woodworm hunts were what they sounded like; a cover-up.

Such a row certainly meant that nothing else would be heard in the vicinity of the hall, and I thought then it was certain the reason for the 'hunts' was hiding another sound.

I did not think of a shot, because a shot is a sharp, uncertain sound that *might* be heard in any sound cover except a lot of other shots.

Then what was the sound that needed such a cover?

Cook did not look round but put out a hand behind her.

'Give me the oven glove,' she said.

'Where is it?' I said.

She straightened and looked round.

'Damn! I thought it was Farne,' she said. 'The old sod's decided to have dinner after all.' She looked for the needed article. 'I'm not so sure I want to stay on, after all. I'd got to like it, but sometimes I get so mad I could kill him.'

She found the glove and went back to the oven.

'I think the shooting was at rabbits,' I said.

She was surprised.

'You do? Why?'

'There was another shot just now and nobody out there.'

I watched her. She watched me.

'Was there? Who?'

'Somebody upstairs,' I said. 'From the window.' She smiled suddenly.

'It must have been somebody shooting woodworm,' she said.

'Does Mr. Cardwell shoot?'

'Only when he's cross. Otherwise he uses a chopper. I tell you, he's as mad — Oh there you are! Where have you been? Didn't you hear? He wants dinner now?'

She had changed her talk to Farne who had just come in with Philips behind him. I noticed Philips had changed his trousers to a pair without stains on them.

'Oh, sir! I am sorry! I had forgotten!' he said, looking at me. 'Do come with me.'

It was elaborate, his drawing attention to his forgetfulness at having left me there. With great gravity he accompanied me back to the supper-room, which was empty.

'The ladies will not be long, sir,' he said, 'but I understand that Mr. Cardwell has now ordered dinner, so they will be changing, you understand, sir.'

'Of course.'

'Shall I get you a drink, sir?'

'No. You had better get things ready, Philips.'

'Very thoughtful of you, sir. If you do fancy anything, please help yourself.'

He went out. There was absolute quiet. For the first time I had an instinctive feeling of being in a trap, and a death trap at that. By force of circumstances I had had to trust Laura with my real business because she knew already what I was.

Cook had been planted and knew anyway, and I felt it was time to wonder if one or both had not dropped hints in the wrong places.

I had been left in the kitchen alone, and now in the supper-room. I began to suspect someone knew I had taken a look round from the dining room and seen the study with the old radio in it.

The curtains weren't drawn over the big windows. I went to them and looked out. I could see no one, but it was difficult, against the silhouettes of the trees not far away, to be sure that nobody was there watching.

I moved to one side as if to get a drink from the table. Instead I passed the table and went to a door by the side of a great stone fireplace. It was unlocked.

There was no noise I could hear inside the house. I opened the door into another room, where the moon shone through windows on to a grand piano but nothing else. I thought this would be the 'gymnasium' where Cardwell did his daily round, for I could see no other furniture at all standing on the polished floor of great wide boards.

I almost closed the door to the supper-room leaving a crack I could see through.

At that time I did not know what to expect because, up till then, there had been no semblance of ordinary behaviour in that household so it was impossible to guess what to expect.

For all I knew, Cardwell might flood the room with home-made poison gas which he was otherwise keeping for the coming revolution.

He would not use a bomb, because that would come up under his own apartment and cause discomfort. Gas clears itself in time, but bomb wreckage doesn't.

Thoughts of murder then were understandable, for by that time I was sure that someone had been killed.

There was the possibility that the Farne inrush and cry of mayhem was a ruse to attract my attention to the fact that there *was* no Mrs. Grobe and no murder outside.

That would assume I had not seen Daffyd burying something in the wood earlier on.

If there had been a murder earlier in the evening and the results disposed of underground, then the uproar later could only have been to suggest to me that the staff were lunatics and that no murder had happened.

But what would have given Cardwell the idea that I would suspect a murder? What would have made him so sure I was thinking along those lines that he had staged a pretence like that?

Who would have given him the idea?

Laura was a dear girl, of whom I was very fond in my way, but I would not have trusted her at all. But what might put her straight with me, was that she knew my idea of trusting her.

The other possibility was Jane Lane, cook and copper's plant. She had been at pains to tell me she had changed her mind about everything since she had been here.

She wouldn't have done that if she'd changed so as to be against me. She must have meant that her sympathies had turned in favour of Cardwell with harm to no one intended, otherwise, as she well knew, things might get uncomfortable for her later.

I could not see how either woman could have put herself into an obviously difficult position by blowing me to Cardwell.

Was there somebody else who suspected why I was there? Or did they all suspect anybody who came?

That was the possibility and part of the game of keeping the world away from this gloomy estate.

But I felt there was something else in the air that was forming a cloud of poison

137

gas over my head.

It is difficult, in such positions of infiltration, to know if, somehow, the spy has been blown from the outside. Usually that is because it is part of a deal above the operator's head. In my case I couldn't see such a situation coming about.

Had I but known it, I had the answer to my problem, and the mystery of the Palace of Iron right behind the door, but one cannot always know these things.

I heard something move in the supper-room. At first I thought it might have been a log shifting on the fire, but remembered the fire had not been lit. It came again, still more like a log shifting in ash, and I realised then that it was coming from the fireplace at the side of the door I stood by.

I opened the door quietly. There was silence, but the candle flames on the tables were swaying slightly as if some faint draught had got to them from somewhere.

The windows appeared to be shut, still, but I could not see the door to the hall. That might have been opened but I should have heard the latch click, and I had heard nothing.

It was not particularly warm and I had wondered why the fire hadn't been lit, but there would be a reason if it was expected that something might come down the chimney.

In such houses the flue from downstairs could easily connect directly with the flue in the upper fireplace.

I waited. It seemed that at last something definite might be about to show.

7

I opened the door wider and looked into the deserted supper-room. The candle flames shook slowly and I thought that perhaps their movement a minute or so before might have been from the crack in my door being ajar rather than from a sudden disturbance in the chimney flue.

The house was quiet, hardly any sound from anywhere until I heard another rustle from the fireplace.

I opened my door still more and went into the supper-room, moving very quietly to try and surprise whatever was happening in the fireplace.

At the time I was aware that if I didn't make some normal noise whoever was listening would suspect I had gone from the room when I should have been still in it, if innocent, as I'd been left there to await the others.

If there was too much silence someone must find out why, but I had the choice of raising a hunt by being quiet or waiting noisily until I was trapped there.

I was quite convinced by then that I was becoming expendable. The idea that it would be too dangerous to kill me because it would bring investigators to find out what had happened, did not hold so much water in my case.

It was known when I started that there was a risk, and if I didn't turn up any more it would be assumed I was dead and that somebody else had better have a go to find out what was wrong in the place.

I was anxious that some attempt would be made on me for two reasons; one, I should at last know where I stood, and two, I was ready for it.

After the pie-eyed shot out of the upper window not long ago I felt that any other attempt would be about as subtle.

There was another rustle in the chimney. I had in my pocket a very small detector for polluted atmospheres giving a warning whether the gas was invisible or without smell. I held it close to the chimney but there was no glow of the warning light.

I began to think in terms of The Speckled Band; a jolly idea of sending a poisonous snake down the chimney, but such schemes are more miss than hit. Snakes or a small army of man-eating ants present too much of a problem for the man who has to collect them up again afterwards.

Perhaps the asinine behaviour in that house to date made me think of equally fatheaded things, but I was quite fixed in my mind to expect anything. It is possible for the Army commander, while preparing his defences against rocket missiles, to be shot by a bow and arrow.

There was another rustle amongst the sticks and logs on the hearth as if something had fallen down the chimney. Now I was close I was certain that was the source of the restlessness in the fireplace, but I did not see anything drop.

I looked up the throat of the flue. It was black. Anything let down there would be invisible if it were all matt black like the soot.

That made me want to peer harder up the flue, but suddenly I thought that might be just what was intended. In such situations of suspicion and possible danger, one should try not to fall for the obvious.

I unbent and moved aside to the door behind which I had hidden before.

As I reached it the whole room was flooded with a brilliant flash of light. Having suspected it, I had my eyes half closed, but even then there was a second of red shock in my retina as I went into the piano room.

I almost closed the door and listened. I heard the main door open. Someone came in quickly then stopped. There was a moment of hesitation, then the intruder went out again, and as he closed the room door I heard him shout something, but the shutting of the door cut off the meaning.

So that was it. A powerful flash guaranteed to blind anyone for several seconds, while someone waiting outside came in and clobbered the blind man.

The slight sounds I had heard were of a soft thin cable being let down with an electric flash of photographic type, but far more powerful, hanging on it ready to blast the watcher's eye. And judging from the effect on my half closed orbs, anyone standing anywhere in the room would have been dazzled for enough seconds to leave him unprepared.

In fact, had I tried to see who had come in by peering through the gap of my door, I shouldn't have been able to, for the face would have been splodged out during those vital seconds by disturbed vision.

So at last there was a definite and clear action which gave the game away as to future intention.

There was a door across the room from me, half covered by the shape of the piano, and that was the only other way out. It seemed to lead into some side passage.

Very soon, a search would begin, starting in the supper-room and I had better get out of range before it did.

I went round the piano and reached the far door. I opened it carefully, praying that it wasn't just a cupboard, but it looked into a passage where a dim, confused light was coming through the glass upper panels of a door on the left.

It seemed a most suitable exit, out into the garden, for I had already made it known I was fond of fresh air, and it might even cool the rush of heated suspicion my absence from the supper-room had certainly roused. Not that such a cooling would do more than delay another shot at the safety of my person.

I went to the door. It was locked and there was no key. The idea of bursting through the glass panes would not help for the key was hardly likely to have been left on the outside. I turned and went along the passage to the right until it joined a major corridor running from the hall on the right to anyone's guess on the left. It was a big house. Iron makers bursting with coin did not waste money on small houses, and rooms were provided for almost any eventuality in the family.

I listened. The same uneasy quiet was everywhere. There was no sign now of the impending dinner. The candles in the hall looked dim, as if someone had borrowed half the sticks for somewhere else.

To the left there was no candle at all. It was obviously the way for me, as he filtered light of the moon struggling through windows darkened with great curtains of ivy, gave just enough glow to see by and hardly enough to be seen by.

I looked back again towards the hall, just to make sure it was clear, and then drew back a little beyond the angle of the wall.

Two figures were approaching the supper-room. The candlelight in the hall came from such an angle that the stairs blocked off the light to the two, so that I could not make out who they were.

They stopped at the door and appeared to be listening, then after a pause went away the way they had come.

That was puzzling, for they already knew I had not been in the room when the flash had gone off and the mauler had come in. Then why listen for me minutes later?

It seemed pointless, unless there was another party in the house unknown to me and the others. Considering the care with which strangers were kept out of the citadel, the very idea of Trojan horsemen marauding under Cardwell's very own stairs was ludicrous.

And yet — why listen for me when you already knew I wasn't there?

I was tempted to go up into the hall and see just who had gone to that door, but turned and went to the left along the corridor. Oddity struck again, for directly opposite all I'd seen already, every door to every room was wide open.

By moonlight struggling through ivy at the windows I could see furniture standing about rather like lonely, neglected ghosts. On the other side, away from the direct moonlight, shapes were vague and hard to distinguish.

I went slowly along, listening carefully as I went. The same quiet persisted. I believed at the end of the corridor I should find another set of stairs, so I went on past the yawning doorways towards the end of the corridor.

My object was to get upstairs and into the dreaded private apartment of the legendary hermit.

In the first place, I wanted to know if he was alive, and if he wasn't, it could be that I might be joining him and the baroness in some Valhalla for impulsive heroes. If the others were keeping up the legend with a corpse, they wouldn't want me to tell anybody.

If he was alive in there he would be angry at seeing me bust in.

He might be very angry indeed. So angry that, having missed me with a senile potshot from the upper window he could point his blunderbuss straight into my gizzard and fire. After that things would be simply dealt with at the farmer's dog meat almost instant disposal unit.

I thought that then with a twisted sense of humour, but I realised the idea was far from extreme. Disposals in acid and other conveyor belt methods have featured in murder cases for ages, and Dafydd's methods of getting rid of unwanted meat were first class.

That was if there had already been a number of murders at this house. I could not help thinking that suspicion of such a thing had been one of the reasons behind urging me to get in here and find out.

But if there had been, how was it none of the victims was reported missing? That someone notices someone is not there is the main reason why murder hunts begin.

Any such reports would have brought official attention to this place in the ordinary way, but none had been made.

So assuming it was a place of murder, what sort of victims had they been?

I turned the corner at the end of the corridor. Still no stairs.

I was about to go on when in the distance I heard the sudden screaming croak of the Klaxon and an accompanying banging of gongs.

And then, as I stood by another open door, I realised these doors might all be left open because this was the area of the furious bug hunts.

And this time one looked like turning into a man hunt.

★ ★ ★

The noise of the hunt beginning started up down the main corridor and rapidly increased in volume. I took a quick stock of my position which looked, from the blocked end of the junction corridor, as if I had trapped myself.

To go into the room beside me would be a temporary hiding-place but I did not know how thorough the search party was and I could not risk it.

Another risk seemed better. I ran across the head of the main corridor into the other passage.

As I did it the noise of the hunters became louder and glancing along towards the hall I saw a party coming towards me, faces lit and moving strangely by flickering candles being carried amongst the pots, pans, pokers, swords, rattles and other bug-scaring devices.

They scared me.

There was shouting amongst the banging and rattling and as I ran across their line of sight I was sure some saw me go.

The noise seemed to increase, the

shouting grew shriller. The branch passage ended like the other, but in a door instead of a wall. Once more I had to pray it wasn't a cupboard, but with my knowledge of old houses I guessed it would be a service door.

The noise increased rapidly, as if the hunters were running along the corridor to reach me. I opened the door. There was a cleaner's cupboard on the left and ahead a flight of bare wooden steps going upwards.

I went through and closed the door behind me. The noise was suddenly damped down and for a moment I felt almost an air lock in my ears at relief from the row.

The small window in that passage delivered only a dim grey light and until I had run to the top of the flight of stairs I did not realise there was a door at the top.

The noise of the hunters was then close behind the door below me. I turned the handle of the stairs door. It was locked. The noise below was shrill then, even through the panels of the service door.

By the side of the stair rail was a shelf

running alongside to the return of the wall above the descending staircase. I saw it as the door below opened and yellow jumping light flooded into the service passage like a fire. The noise rushed up at me as I stepped on to the shelf.

I flattened my back against the wall and went cautiously along towards the return. I reached that as the candles came almost directly below me.

The meaningless chanting and singing went on, though there were no words. I got on to the return shelf and stayed perfectly still with my back against the wall.

Someone detached from the party below and ran up the stairs to the door. He tried it, then shouted.

'It's locked!'

He turned and faced down the stairs his features illuminated by the candles below. By raising his eyes he could have seen me though the light did not shine directly on me.

Still the chanting and shouting did not stop. He ran down again. There was a disturbed note in the row, and then it began to go away out through the service door again, but stayed even louder it seemed to me.

I crabbed back to the top of the stairs and then, while the retreating din was still high, bust the door with a flat-foot kick and went through as it crashed open.

I shoved the door shut again and stood in a sudden peaceful quiet of the upper landing.

Grey moonlight filtered through a window on the left, but the hanging ivy was so shaggy it looked like a half-closed eye.

The noise below sounded faint, and then suddenly it stopped altogether.

It did occur to me then that, although it might be a device for covering up other noises, it might also be a ploy to make one accustomed to these outbreaks so that when it really did cover up an unwanted noise I shouldn't notice.

One of the troubles with that place was that every oddity seemed to have several explanations, one mad and one reasonably villainous.

The quiet again descended. I heard

nobody moving anywhere. The preparations for dinner seemed to have been abandoned. From what I had seen, the inmates of the place must eat in their own rooms with smuggled tuck, otherwise they must have gone mad with this start-stop-never-a-bite routine.

I began to go along the corridor. The carpet was thick as turf, a purposeful noise killer, perhaps for the benefit of the hermit who liked silence which he could split on sudden impulse with his klaxon and other devices.

The landing right ahead was lit only by the glow of the few candles which had been left down in the hall, and nothing else. It was enough to shed a little light to reflect on the gilt lining of the door panels which I saw as I passed them. I thought such splendour must indicate the residence of the Superboss.

On the splendid carpet it was possible to walk quite normally without making any sound. It was also possible to listen for anyone about and so be prepared for a surprise. By looking forward and backward I could see if anyone was about, and by doing that and listening I felt I must be alone in the world.

At one of the doors I stopped and decided to take a risk. The ornate gold lever handles were a temptation to me when any one might unlock the secret of the house.

That thought turned my mind into another direction. That house had been built because of the ironworks down by the river. Suppose the real heart of the matter still lay hidden down in that impressive ruin?

The idea occurred because it was instinctive and had the right feeling, but I might never get into this house again if I found the answer down by the river.

Very carefully, making no noise I tried a handle of one door. It was a beautifully made lock I could tell by the feel, and well greased, also, so that without making the slightest noise I turned it fully and found the door locked.

I went on to the next and found it the same.

It was then that I heard some activity down in the hall, a moving about as if once more, the constantly delayed dinner was proposed.

I tried the last door before the corridor opened up into the landing. The handle turned, the door started to give. I hesitated, holding the door still shut.

There is always a doubt about the one door unlocked, and that is it may be the one that is guarded inside. And if anyone was inside watching, they would see the lever handle turn.

Slowly, very carefully, I let the handle go back into the latched position, released my hold and stepped aside and backed into the recess of the next door along. From there I watched the unlocked doorway.

Nothing happened for as long as a minute while the footfalls and clink of dishes sounded from the hall below, and then a faint seam of light appeared on the inside edge of the architrave of the unlocked door.

Someone was opening it from inside, but very slowly, very steadily. I watched that slowly brightening line of light with one eye as I peered round the edge of my niche.

Someone spoke down in the hall; a woman asking about dinner. Philips replied. It all sounded so normal. Even the light from the door stopped brightening and stayed still. There were footsteps walking away again then silence below.

I moved my head out further and saw the vertical band of light quite steady and unchanging, as if the hand behind the door held the door steadily at the point.

Then suddenly, the light disappeared, but in the instant of it happening I saw it had not been cut by the door shutting.

The light had been turned off inside the room. That indicated the man inside suspected or knew someone was outside watching.

I wondered then how he knew I was still waiting.

Did he suspect a stranger of trying to open his door. There were others in the house, and if the man inside suspected a stranger, why did he not bang his gong as usual?

The thought came that the man inside should not have been there anyway; that he was as much a usurper as I was.

Already I had had the idea that the people who had tried the door of the supper room might be strangers. This second suggestion of it came on the heels of the first, and raised a number of questions only one of which really counted.

If an outsider had got in, there must have been an inside means of helping him, which meant one of the hermit's staff. That would have explained why two had gone to the door of the supper room; the intruder and his inside helper.

I wished very much I had somehow managed to get my dear little Smith & Wesson into that ivy-ridden pile but till then it would have given more away than it could have saved — but not now.

The time had come to play the guess to the limit. I stepped out of my hole and went quickly to the next door. It proved to be on the point of opening further as I saw from a faint upright band of moonlight on the inside wall of the room.

I shouldered it in. There was an immediate resistance, which collapsed so suddenly it almost let me go headlong into the gloom. The man behind the door had fallen in the way of its fully swinging open. I went round the edge and looked down at the sprawling figure on the light carpet.

I grabbed the body by the collar and hauled it up almost into a kneeling position.

'Don't give me away!'

The plea was made in a whisper and it was a woman's tone. She remained perfectly still on her knees while I listened, but heard nothing of anybody else in the place. I bent to look at the pale woman's face which was turned up to mine.

'Who are you?' I said very quietly.

'Mrs. Grobe,' she said. 'Don't hit me!'

I relaxed my grip and signed her to get up. She did so shakily, but I did not let her lean on me and kept my grip steady on her coat.

'You were shot at?' I said.

'Yes. I'll kill him before he can kill me. Let me go. I want to get out of here.'

'How did you get in?'

'I can't tell you that.'

'It might hurt somebody else?'

'Yes.'

I looked around. There was hardly any furniture in the room.

'Is this his apartment?'

She shook her head.

'This is the dead one,' she said.

'What do you mean? Is he dead?'

'No — hers. She is dead. The baroness. She died.'

'And no one lives here now?'

'No. They wouldn't.'

'Then why did you come here?'

'It was something I wanted. It is mine. It was stolen.'

She was almost childlike in her answers, like a woman suffering from shock or great grief.

'Was it yours — this thing that was stolen?'

'No. Not mine then.'

'Whose was it?'

'My son's. She took it from him.'

'And you came to get it back?'

'I could not find it.' She sounded almost as if she would cry.

160

'Have you tried before?'

'I come to the farm now and then. It is the only way I can get — near.'

'You say your son lost this — thing here.'

'No. She stole it.'

'The baroness?'

'Yes.'

'But that was a long time ago?'

'No. Not long long.'

'Three — four years?'

She shook her head again.

'Not three — four months.'

8

'Do you mean the baroness was alive three months ago?' I said.

The woman looked nervously all round the room as if someone might be listening to us, then nodded.

'Are you sure?'

'Of course. He went to see her. He was in trouble. He would not say what, but he took this thing to her to pay for her help.'

'What was it?'

'I don't know. I only know the box it was in.'

'And did she help your son?'

'I suppose so. I never saw him more.'

'You mean that she helped by getting him away — out of the country?'

'Yes.'

The first real piece of information came out as if the woman did not realise the importance of what she was saying.

'What was your son? What did he do?'

'He was on a paper, but he wrote about

a gang who didn't like it and they were going to kill him.'

'Oh. I thought you meant he was in trouble with the police.'

'Well — ' she hesitated, ' — he weren't in trouble with them, exactly, but he couldn't go to them.'

The information was important, but time was passing and the search would go on in a minute and standing about in one place was too dangerous to go on with.

'How did you get in?' I said quickly.

'There's stairs inside the study wall. Comes direct up in here from outside. She had them put. Secret way for herself. Over there. The cupboard by the chimney.'

She was a mine of information of an unexpected sort.

'Who shot at you?'

'Me? When?'

'Out in the garden. When you came.'

I saw her shake her head.

'Tweren't me,' she said. 'I said it was just now because I know it was meant for me, but they mistook for somebody else.'

For the first time her evidence began to

shake. She had changed an important part of it, and that made me wonder about the reliability of the rest of it.

'You'd better go,' I said. 'They are looking for somebody.'

'They's always lookin'. Crazy it is. Now and again I come with veges and there's banging and shouting like they were all witches screaming for the devil. Makes me want to scream myself.'

There was no sound of a hunt-up at the moment, but again I felt it prudent to break off and move.

There was just one question I wanted her to answer.

'If this is the baroness's apartment, where is his?'

'I never saw it. It's a room with no doors. That's all I know.'

She turned suddenly and went to the cupboard beside the fireplace. Her movement took me by surprise. It was as if she had heard something, or sensed it, and I hadn't.

I watched as she went into the cupboard and shut the door behind her, then I stood by the room door listening. I heard nothing when I opened it. The old haunting quiet was back.

It was broken as I heard someone walking along the passage below and into the hall. A door was opened, then shut again, and there was no more noise.

It sounded as if all hunts had been abandoned. As if they didn't care I was loose in the house or even outside it. That could mean one of two things.

The first meaning could be that they were all innocent and my escape would not matter at all.

The second was that it didn't matter if I did get out of the house because I would never get out of the estate around it.

The second was the more likely.

I went out into the corridor again and closed the white door behind me.

The search was now to be very hard if I were to look for a room without a door at all, so first of all it was best to ponder what she had meant by such a strange description.

It could mean that she had just never seen a door where she knew the room to be. It could mean that the room had no door as such but a trapdoor in the ceiling or through the floor.

The trouble with the second idea was how the gongs and klaxons sounded so well outside the room if there was no way the higher registers could get out of it and sound the frequent alarms. A boom-boom effect would not have sounded like the row I had heard.

I went on to the landing. It was spacious, of square shape running back to windows overlooking the woods at the back of the house. I had noted its shape before, but not in connection with looking for a room that wasn't there.

Thinking back, I had seen one of the women running across the corridor leading to my room and going into a door opposite the one she had come out of.

I entered the corridor and tried the first door on the right. It opened. I took it cautiously in case anyone was behind it but there was no reaction and I opened the door and went in.

I went into an empty room. Empty not only of people or any sort of animal but also any sort of furnishings. The boards, the windows were all bare.

Yet I had seen the cook rush into this room when summoned by demanding gongs.

There was another door on the left hand wall beyond the fireplace. I went across, opened it and looked into the adjoining room.

It was bare as the first. I looked at the ceilings of both rooms and neither had any opening. The same applied to the bare, boarded floors.

I thought of the famous Victorian device of the turnable fireplace and tried each room one after the other, but if they had such tricks in them, I saw no sign of the means whereby they were made to do it.

I stood in that connecting doorway and thought, and I also thought that the company below — or wherever they were — were taking no interest at all in my whereabouts.

Such ignorance indicated that they knew I wouldn't find anything anyway. Then was there nothing of Cardwell in the house after all? Was he dead? How was it that the woman had said the baroness had been alive only three months before when it was supposed to be three years since she died?

And the story of the son frightened of a gang. The baroness was supposed to have got him out of the country, and yet the baroness had been as much a recluse as her husband.

Then how had she connections which enabled her to get people out? Such contacts need to be live and right up-to-date, otherwise one can deliver an escaper into the hands of the enemy and not know that, not only has your protegee been sold, but yourself as well.

And no one was allowed to visit the house, and that was too well-known to be a myth.

But there was the baroness's secret stairway which Mrs. Grobe knew about and used. Yet there again, one would have to reach it, and without the excuse of bringing produce from time to time, one would almost certainly be spotted, as indeed, Mrs. Grobe had been, though owing to confusion in the moonlight someone else had been mistaken for her at the critical moment.

That had been very lucky for her, unless the shot had been as bad as that popped at me from the upstairs window.

As I stood there in a room of brightening moonlight and nothing else, I began to feel I had the answer to the Cardwell enigma forming in my mind, but I needed to ask questions of one of the staff, and that was now very difficult, if not impossible.

I went out into the corridor again and looked at the opposite door, the one from which I had seen the cook come out.

It was unlocked. In the normal course of events a cook should be about in the kitchen when dinner was being served, but as I had learned, there was no normal course of events in this place, therefore I opened the door very carefully indeed.

There was no light burning inside, but the moon was getting friendlier all the time, as if the day-long overcast was clearing.

The light showed a quite handsome bedroom in a state of chaos. The bedclothes had been pulled half on the floor; garments sprawled everywhere, on the carpet, over chairs, even over mirrors, as if the woman occupier had stripped, throwing everything about, pulled the bed almost off, then had rushed out in the nude.

The whole room looked as if anger still seethed in it.

It was such a mess that for a moment I did not see the naked woman spilt on to the floor beside the bed. She was sprawled there face down, half obscured by the flowing mess of the bedclothes.

I crossed to where she lay. There was a torch on the bedside table and I used it to see who she was. I lifted one shoulder so that her head turned slightly.

Jane Lane, cook and planted agent, was dead.

I lifted her shoulder more until her back was against the side of the bed. There was a two-two shot between the breasts which looked as if it had driven right into the heart. There was not a great deal of blood.

So somehow she had been sprung. Her

murder made quite clear something that had not been certain before, and it was that this whole business was desperate and perfectly callous in defending itself.

I let the body go down again and straightened.

She had been killed not so long before, but something had happened that evening that had blown her cover and I wondered what it had been.

Perhaps something she had said during the interrogation by Philips and Trellis in the kitchen which had followed the incident in the garden.

It was more than likely that had been the occasion of cook giving herself away. Not long after she had been murdered in her room.

A shot had also been taken at me, but it had been such a bad one I could not decide whether it had been muffed or was intended as a warning not to interest myself in local events.

Finding cook suggested it had been no warning.

She might have been shot from the doorway and had half turned as she fell.

She could have been entangled in the bedclothes as she went down amongst them.

I could see no point in any murderer arranging a scene by spilling everything about in a house where they were all in villainy together.

It must be the first of the spy eliminations.

The second one seemed to be standing there looking at it.

★ ★ ★

Carefully, I went out into the corridor, looked, listened and could make out nothing but the slight sounds of a meal being served; the measured pace along the downstairs passage from kitchen quarters to the supper room, the rattle of a glass, table tools, dish-cover. Not at all the sounds of a household which has just shot the cook.

I closed the door and went into my room at the end of the passage. I went in more carefully than I had done in entering any room up to then.

It was silent in there and the moonlight through the window gave it almost a magical glow. I used the ex-cook's torch and made sure the room was empty, then went through to the fantasy room.

I could see no one in there, but the shadows thrown by the outrageous bric-à-brac made sighting difficult. The whole room, however, was dead quiet, so much so I thought I would have heard anyone breathing.

The curtains were drawn, so I went to the big window and pulled them back to let in the moonlight. Then I turned off the torch and looked slowly round.

This room had no door to the passage.

The door to the bathroom, which was the first along on that side, was quite a way away from mine in terms of feet, but even so, taking the width of the fantasy room and the distance to the bathroom door, any secret room in between was going to be very small. By their nature, secret rooms can't be large or the discrepancy of the outside measurements would make them obvious.

But would the millionaire recluse live in a cupboard?

Taking into account all appearances, the man might be barmy enough for that.

The banging of gongs also did not fit with a sealed-up room. The sounds were too rich, bright and clear even in a house of that size.

There was the possibility of an electronic device, but to any normal ear an electronic device sounds like an electronic device, despite claims of fidelity which might have been said to Cynara, as an excuse and not a claim.

I used the torch again and went round the walls but found no trace of an opening anywhere.

A room with no doors. It could mean a well or the top of a narrow tower.

And then it occurred to me that perhaps Cardwell wasn't in a room at all. But then why should the woman have specified a room and made the point that it was a peculiar room in that it had no doors?

There was no point in standing in there guessing. Sooner or later the interested parties would come into it and I should be clobbered if I was caught there.

And still I couldn't resist the temptation to look round once more. This time I started by shining the torch on the ceiling, painted over with erotica of Germanic crudity and heavy shadowing so that parts of it looked as if it were modelled in relief.

I listened again for any sound from the bedroom, then got up on a sofa which brought me within reach of the surface of the ceiling. I kept the torchlight as near as possible so that it gave no reflection outside the room.

The ceiling decoration had been so heavily daubed that there were raised ridges of paint left, and this gave it the effect of being in relief.

Looking closer at the ceiling painting it become clearer that the work was not just for entertainment but also to cover something up. The heavy daubings could confuse the eye if some opening was there in the flat ceiling.

I was directly underneath a massive Brunhilde wearing only the legs of a suit of armour apparently running down on to me from out of the general scene. I noticed a dissimilarity in the symmetry of the formidable chest, reached up and pressed the left nipple which seemed to be protruding.

There was a click. I thought, 'Eureka!' but no trapdoor opened. Instead there was a sharp hiss, like escaping steam, and then the most awful din started up somewhere in the house.

I had heard it before; the gongs, the klaxon, the bells, clangers, rattles and cymbals, but the fact of having started it myself made the whole thing sound like a timpani accompaniment to the Last Trump.

The hiss, like escaping steam and the full fury of the unmusical racket connected in my head with a complaint from the invisible Cardwell that all the hot water was used up.

He had got an old fairground steam organ fixed up somewhere specially devised to let loose the maximum din on the pressing of steam buttons, strategically located in rooms used by him.

It was difficult to guess what would happen now, but it was clear I had better get out of that room fast.

There was a possibility that the housemates might know that the alarm was not supposed to sound and I might be the only one about who could have operated it.

The bedroom window was still open. I got out of it and climbed down the ivy to the ground, a far from silent procedure but as the steam organ was still at crescendo I thought those inside the house would be unlikely to hear me.

For a few seconds I waited and listened until the steam organ stopped, but I did not hear any answering din from the roused hunters.

That seemed to indicate they knew the alarm had not been genuine.

I ran to the corner of the house. My vehicle still stood there, just out of direct sight of the front door, as I had thoughtfully left it. I ran on and opened its unlocked door.

By that time, suspected as I was, and even under pursuit, I decided I had gone long enough without adequate protection.

Leaning in, I shifted the gear lever into a position it should not have had, then pulled up a corner of the carpet, lifted the trap unlocked by the gear shift and took out my thirty eight revolver and a small box of spare rounds. I closed everything again and turned to go back towards the woods and the valley.

As I started, somebody shouted from the front doorway. I ran fast. Before I reached the comparative camouflage of the woods, two shots were fired behind me. They sounded like twelve bore shot, but the aimer didn't seem to have the range.

The man in the upper window hadn't any idea of the range, either.

Bit by bit, things were linking together. If only the whole lot would get into a chain formation it could shorten the period of my suffering.

In the journey through the wood I went nowhere near the paths. Now and again I stopped and looked back. I thought I saw a figure here and there but picking shadows amongst those hundreds of trees made it too difficult to be sure.

The only thing I could be sure of was that having been seen to run away from the car and then been shot at, they were after me by some means or other.

I got to the edge of the drop down on to the old ironworks which showed clearly below me, every part picked out sharply by the brightening moon.

It was then necessary to turn along until the track was reached in order to slope down to the hard below. Anyone following me would be watching the track because it was the only way down for anyone but an experienced climber.

To show myself on the track would be to get a backful of shot if not my head shot off.

I was not under any delusion that murder was difficult to cover up in these parts, and in the back of my mind I kept having the idea that there had been quite a number.

The son of Mrs. Grobe had been 'helped out of the country' but cutting his head off and using the remains in the dogmeat boiler would have had roughly the same effect.

The business of instigating a shoot-out is never a good one. A gun is most effective when you don't have to use it; its effectiveness is not put to the test, but its moral value is. A man with a gun may win when he can't even shoot; two gunmen shooting can't tell who'll win.

Considerations of that sort made me decide to take a long way round, by turning left away from the track and going down the further slope — if there still was one handy,, and if not, then search further on still until one was found. The works site had been scooped out of the hill, forming a cliff, so it couldn't be that far to a gentler descent.

So I thought. Somebody else had thought of it before me.

As I went towards the promised slope, I saw a movement in the trees ahead of me.

That someone was on that flank meant they had known, roughly, the course I was taking, and convinced me that to go back to the old cart road would be suicide.

The mould between the trees was thick

as several carpets and almost silent to walk on. I began to retreat from the cliff edge and to work my way round to the left to bring myself up behind the person cutting me off there.

In doing it I had to watch all round me and move from tree to tree smartly between each look. I saw no one move. That meant they had lost me and were waiting to see where I would turn up.

I realised that I might be up against Daffyd, an obviously experienced wood-craftsman, and the rest, though not experienced in the same way, would certainly know the ways of that wood, which I had to guess at.

Gradually I worked round almost to the spot where I had seen a figure move. I stopped by a tree and watched very carefully. For a while I saw nothing move at all, and then I heard someone whisper.

'You won't 'scape them by yourself. Take advice. The bushes to your left. In the middle a shaft comes up. Rough going down, but better than death staying up.'

In such a situation, any apparently pleasant relief can be a trap, but if this was, then it was the most idiotic one I had ever come across. Who would believe it, put as it had been?

Traps are set with care, and with special care for the invitations which lead into them. This was no such lure but plain signal to take it or leave it — 'it's nothing to me either way'.

In fact I saw the figure walk away parallel with the river valley as if no longer interested in my fate.

It was difficult, in that light and with the trees all round, to make out who it was. He seemed to be going away with the woodsman's knowledge that he was keeping the trees behind him as a protection.

From what I saw it could have been anyone, though naturally for several reasons I thought of the old man of the woods, though why he should do me any good — except out of spite of the household — I could not think.

The sound of his going stopped as he went out of earshot. As it died away I heard other sounds, as if the hunt, having lost sight of me, was starting a beat.

It looked a perfect trap except for the unusual behaviour of the informant. I should have to move anyway and I might as well try the suggested opening as fall down it in making a run for it.

I went very carefully to the clump of bushes. As I went I heard a soft, sharp whistle as if my movement had been spotted. More and more it looked and sounded like a snare.

Ducking down by the bushes I made out their main shapes against the moonlight filtering down through the trees and pushed my shoulder in between two of them. They scratched the cloth of my jacket but I went slowly so that the noise was kept soft.

Slowly I got in amidst the clump and felt the ground with my hand. The edge of a hole was there all right, and more than that, it was roughly lined with stone like a vent from some part of the works below.

The sounds of agitation following became unmistakable, as if they had now guessed where I was heading. It was the last push I needed. I stuffed my gun into my trousers pocket so that falling and banging about should not move it and make it fall out without the best of bad luck, then went over the edge.

My feet didn't meet anything until I kicked the side of a slope below me. A few loose stones rattled away, and I thought I had sunk into a trap with its own built-in sound warning system.

But the stonework did not last long. I begun to slither down an earth slope inside a sort of tube so I could touch both sides with my hands. The slide was not too fast or steep.

I even had time to see moonlight filtering through some sort of hole at the bottom beyond my feet.

It was a relief. At least it showed I was not going to end up lost inside some long-disused boiler.

9

The slide down that vent was not hard going, for the sides were crumbly earth, easy and slow to slide on and the show of moonlight below was a relief.

The drop was in fact, not that far — about seventy feet in all, I suppose — too far to fall but fairly easy down this underground lift.

Near the bottom I dug my heels in to slow the rate of descent. A lot of earth I dug up thus tumbled away and rolled out on a stone floor below me. If anyone was there waiting it would be a useful signal.

I increased the dig and stopped altogether by pressing against the tunnel sides with my hands.

The bits of earth stopped going down. I listened but could hear only the rushing of water over the rocks upstream of the works. I got the gun out of my pocket and then slid very slowly down, trying to disturb the earth as little as possible.

The moon was bright after the dark of the vent. It seemed to have been some sort of fuel chute for it landed in a stone walled enclosure the stonework now broken and fallen away in heaps. It was just outside the main walls of the works, which still stood though, of course, parts of them had also fallen away. Some of the old iron roof trusses were still up there on top of the walls but the condition of stability must have been I judged, very dodgy.

A crack and slight movement in a wall and the lot would topple and crash down. But it was a still night.

I looked along to the end of the main building to where the ground sloped down to the river, but saw no one taking that way down.

The other way I saw the cart track coming down on to the hard, but no one was using that either. Not a sign of any persons, hunters or otherwise.

Perhaps my followers thought I was just escaping and had no reason to come down to the old ruins, therefore they still kept hunting the woods.

That is what I hoped was happening, for I wanted to have a look round the once great ironworks. The main part of the works seemed too open for any secret part to be around there, so I started looking for the office, the counting-house, the place where all the imports had been booked in and all the exports booked out.

They should be down by the quay where the office staff would have been able to see what was going on the barges and what was coming off.

The trouble was that to get out there would be to be exposed to anyone watching from above, so I kept along the shadow of the works walls, frequently taking a look back up into the woods, but seeing nothing of the hunters.

There should have been six of them, but I hoped that if Laura was with them she would be only the Florence Nightingale of the party, ready to embalm my violated corpse. I don't know why I thought that, when I knew she would sell me up if there was enough money in it for her.

I got to the front of the works quite

close to the landing stage. On the right, set with their backs against the cliffs I saw what must have been the offices. Their small paned, iron-framed windows looked intact. The main door stood half open.

To reach that building meant crossing the open space where the cart track came down. I took another look up to the woods from the nearest point of cover from the open space, but could see no activity up there.

It would have been better if the moon had gone in for a few seconds, but there was now nothing for it to go in behind, so I had to risk a dash.

I dashed, having checked there were no loose flagstones or other spare parts lying in the way I chose. I reached the door of the offices.

There was no activity but the rushing of the water on the rocks upstream. Though that noise could have covered a small sound it would not have covered a shot.

From the corner of the offices I could see up the stone track to the woods and still there was nothing to give away any person there.

The door was wide enough for me to go in without shoving it, which I thought might make a row. The moon filtered in through the dirty windows, but it showed clearly enough the old office equipment with its high, sloping desks, stools, letterpress, a clock over the iron fireplace and an old roll window calendar with the year 1878 still showing in the dusty gap at the bottom.

I thought it was odd I should be able to see that so clearly in the filtered moonlight, so went to look. The glass was dusty but not caked up. The rest of the furniture was dusty, but not very thickly.

Perhaps the ancient millionaire came here to condole with the ageing pieces and ponder on the lost past.

There was a door, half open, leading to the next office, and ruminating on the first office the idea did occur that I might soon find a wooden sled called Rosebud.

There was nothing in the next office but a safe, quite a big old thing, about five feet high. It was a curious sort of thing to leave behind there, and like the rest of the furniture, it didn't look as dirty as it should have done.

It had a keyhole and a big brass turnkey handle. There was a paper lying on the floor in front of it as if dropped when somebody had hurriedly taken a lot of things out.

I bent and picked it up. It had laid face down, and as I turned it over I saw some typed symbols arranged in sections vertically and on the left hand side the photograph of a man.

Cook's torch was useful then and I used it to see the details on the sheet. The whole thing was a photostat.

The items typed down were in code but the photograph was clear.

I recognised the face of that man, though I had not seen him for some two years. His name was — usually — Garson and he had been a member of a crackpot lot of anarchists who had either disbanded or gone underground.

The safe was of considerable age and I thought that with luck and the ingenious lock picker in my penknife I might get its big door open, but to start with I tried the big brass handle to get the feel of the mechanism.

The action did more than give the feel. It nearly opened the safe.

Now when on the prowl as I was then, I am always suspicious of things I want to look into being unlocked. Booby traps are made that way.

I let the sheet of paper fall where it had been, and as I did it I heard someone come very softly into the other office.

There was a cupboard on the wall opposite the window, its door slightly open. I went into it and pulled the door almost to with one hand while holding my gun steadily with the other.

The sound of movement stopped and there was only the distant background rushing of the water to be heard. Then movement began again.

Someone came into the second office and stopped in front of the safe. It was a man, but I could not see well enough to make out who.

He stayed still looking at the safe, his head cocked as if listening. Twice he turned and looked back through the doorway into the other office.

He was either very frightened or plain nervous of the dark and everything else.

He saw the paper on the floor but did nothing about it. Instead he brought a key from his pocket and stuffed it into the safe lock. Of course, when he tried to unlock it, the key would not turn.

He grew agitated at that, pulled the key out, held it up against the moonlit window to make sure the pattern was not blocked up with anything, then repeated his unlocking attempt.

It occurred to him suddenly that the safe might be unlocked and he tried the handle, which turned. He let it go and looked back into the other office again, as if made more nervous still by his discovery.

He dusted his hands together, then grasped the handle and turned it. He pulled the heavy door open and bent so that his head must have gone inside. I could not see from the door then cut off my sight of all of him but his feet.

I heard a 'plop'. It wasn't a silenced

gun and nothing seemed to happen as a result.

Then I saw the feet begin to shift on the floor, sliding, it seemed, against each other, then outwards from each other and then the man tumbled out in a heap, but the safe door still cut off the main picture from me.

I waited. Nothing moved. I got my small detector from my pocket. It showed a very faint trace of gas.

There was no movement visible from the man on the floor. So there had been a trap in the unlocked safe.

Opening the cupboard door a little more I tested the air again. The warning signal was stronger on my instrument. I decided to wait and let it disperse before going out.

As I almost shut the door I heard somebody else come into the offices. They weren't being quiet, but came tramping through and then stopped.

'There he is, look.'

It was Daffyd.

I pushed the door open an inch and watched the big man standing there, his gun slanting down under his arm. He looked at the man on the floor and then stirred him with his boot.

'What's the matter with him? Fainted?'

'Dead,' said somebody I could not see.

'But what's he doing here — ?'

I saw the farmer suddenly pulled back out of the room. Then I heard just Daffyd's voice.

'Gas? Why didn't you say before? I might ha' gone down too!'

They crunched out again.

If the earlier part of my visit had been puzzling, this was worse. If Daffyd had been hunting me he would not have crunched about like a brigade of Guards on a parade ground.

If he had had anything to do with the booby-trapped safe he wouldn't have gone in there like that without a mask, so on the basis of these two facts he seemed innocent of any ill-wish towards me.

But the person behind him had known about the gas and knew the sniffer would be dead, so he was evil; but a single word uttered sharply, almost in a hiss, was impossible to identify.

The place was quiet again. I opened the door wider and used the detector. It showed only the faintest trace of gas.

I used a handkerchief over my mouth and nose and went out into the room.

The safe was empty but for an aerosol can arranged like a spray gun for do-it-yourself paint scratch repairs. It pointed at the safe door and there was a string tabbed to the back of the safe door, running in, over a shelf bar, down to another, then up to the spray trigger.

I looked at the man on the floor. His face was upturned, his mouth open. Farne, the phantom shoe-polisher, was dead.

But what had he been looking for? How had he not guessed there would be a trap here?

It seemed certain then that the office safe had been the store for incriminating documents, possibly revealing the whole mysterious business of the house of the Iron Maker.

I went out into the other office and stood at the door, watching the water go by, sparkling in the moonlight.

A number of old surmises came to my mind, going back to what had seemed a wild idea that the place was the centre of a murder company, killing people who would leave no one to ask after them.

Spies are such people, and foreign spies would be offensive to the exaggerated patriotism of Cardwell and the late baroness.

I felt the fact that Mrs. Grobe had said the dear departed was not as late as everybody had supposed; at that stage it did not seem to matter.

But was the business of attracting spies to this place, and then playing Sweeney Todd on them, such an expensive business? Why had the investments been shuffled around to cover up substantial outgoings?

It happens, even, that there are people who will actually pay to have inconvenient spies disposed of.

And then another curious point. Stocking the house with a staff of fine women was supposed to have taken place because the baroness had died and freed Cardwell from obligations to her dignity.

Had the baroness joined in with the employing of such a bunch? If so, why had none of them given any doubt that the baroness was dead?

And why pick such people for the business of running a slaughterhouse?

The suspicious part to my mind, was that such an organisation of slaying traitors might be attributed to the looney fervour of the ancient man and his belligerent frau, but that seemed to me more like the reasoning in a plot for a musical comedy or even an outright farce.

But suppose the couple were dead, nobody outside knew that fact, and a wipe-out business was being carried on under cover of the public assumption that Cardwell was mad and that was all that was really the matter at that house?

And of course, up till then, nobody outside did know anyone had been murdered.

There should have been a link which pulled all the happenings together, and once I had thought Daffyd must be that link, but just now I had seen clearly that he was not.

Again I wondered about the senseless repetition of the bughunts to which everybody rushed at the command 'Gong-and-Klaxon'.

One point was that I had noticed they seemed to be confined to certain defined areas of the house as if woodworm flew only in certain directions.

It was as daft as the careful watching to see no strangers got into the house while a back way built by the baroness would let anyone in easily.

Or the cook fleeing at the command of the gongs, into an empty room across the corridor.

Or the dinner that never came.

Or the pretentious nonsense of my sandwich and the buffoonery of Tasting the Guinness in the silver cup.

It was as if these people had been rehearsed by some unseen director.

Rehearsed.

Nobody put a foot wrong. They each played a part for all it was worth. Farne's constant boot polishing, the butler's ponderous activities; Mrs. Fox always with a file of figures; Miss Lewson keeping her secretarial activities close to the conversation; even Laura explaining in detail how she kept up her legal knowledge —

The solicitor in the town. He was the only admitted outsider who could know what was going on because, even if Laura did not tell him, he could work it out from the sort of advice she needed.

There was the possibility that the Cardwells had died and the women had worked up a fraud syndicate to operate the fortune without it being too obvious to the brokers. Hence an accountant, a part-time solicitor, and a secretary to hold them together.

But Mrs. Grobe said the baroness had been alive when her son had disappeared a few months before, so even if Cardwell had died years before, the baroness hadn't and it was difficult to imagine anyone with her history being diddled by a gang of women.

But there was one other small incident which I had not, perhaps, taken enough notice of.

The old man of the woods. He had

been dozing in the study chair. Also he had referred to the inmates as lunatics or nearly so.

And last, he had helped me get away from them by showing me that vent.

So that if anyone had a true idea of what had gone on in that house it could have been that old man.

The trouble was that he only appeared from time to time and I had no idea where to find him.

The idea that he might be Cardwell gone back to Nature was unlikely because it was certain that the inmates, as he called them, would never let him roam about talking to people like me, if Cardwell he was.

Nor would they have dismissed him as some soft-headed old fool who talked to rabbits.

I heard somebody tramping about on the hard as if they had been standing for some time and had suddenly decided to move.

There was a small glass screen to the left of the door and I could see dimly in the dusty sheet as in a black mirror.

A man was walking on the edge of the quay looking over into the water.

It looked like Daffyd. His gun was broken and under his arm. There was something in his attitude which made me feel I should take a chance.

When he came opposite the door, I spoke just loud enough for him to hear above the rushing of the upstream water.

'Here.'

He turned his head, cocked as if puzzled, and then he saw me in the doorway. I had my pistol ready but did not hold it so that he could see it. He saw me and started to walk towards me, still with the broken gun drooping under his arm.

'They were looking for you,' he said, halting.

'I thought they were wood pixies,' I said. 'They didn't say anything.'

He looked at my feet.

'You've been in there?' he said, but it hardly sounded a question.

'Yes.'

'They killed him. Little Farney. Now what the bloody hell's the sense of that?'

'Who do you mean killed him?'

'That bloody lot of hags up there in the house.' He raised his head but looked aside along the wall. 'He was a good lad. They made a fool of him. 'Polish the boots,' they said, 'Polish the boots, look!' They got him daft. He meant no harm, that lad. He just wished to know what happened to Him.'

'The old man? Cardwell?'

'He said he would go and find out. I said he was a daring fool, they would see through his game, but he said he must know because he loved the Old Man. He was like a dog sometimes, he would know when there was trust in a person, and he would know when not. He was a good lad.'

'What do you think happened to the Old Man?'

'I reckon they sawed him up.'

'You were burying something in the woods this evening. I saw you.'

'I was.' He still didn't look at me.

'What was it?'

'Meat they'd left to go off. So 'twas said. In a sack, it all smells alike.'

'That wasn't unusual?'

'The orders went to me. Then I gets the sacks full of smell. They says he kept ordering, then stopping and it went off, so they said. So 'bury it' they says. So I do.

'Fore that they says, 'Why don't you put en in your boiler and sell for dog meat?' I says you can't sell meat gone off.'

'Do you think it was your meat gone off?'

He looked at me then for almost the first time.

'I don't think otherwise,' he said slowly. 'I don't want I should end up in my own dog meat.'

10

'What makes you think they killed the old man?' I said.

The farmer turned his head slowly towards me.

'Well, where is he? He hasn't been seen for seasons. Farne looked for him. I told you that. He looked and didn't see him. Mrs. Grobe knew a way in. She didn't find him.'

'She said the baroness was alive a few months ago.'

He shook his head.

'No she weren't. I know she died some three year back. Some such as that. I reckon she saw one of the women acting like the baroness. If you wants to frighten a natural, or make 'em believe something, you show 'em what they think is dead. Either they scare or they think they was wrong in the first place. Mrs. Grobe thought she was wrong in the first place.'

'What was the purpose of pretending

the baroness was alive when it was generally known she was dead?'

He stared at me for some seconds.

'You asks me difficult questions,' he said. 'Them things you ask is what has puzzled me for a long time and I ain't got no answer. 'Tis a madhouse, to all looks from the outside, but there ain't no mad people in there. They knows what they's doing, and all the mad play is to stop you seeing what goes on.'

'You know that much,' I said. 'Do you know of any reason why they should cover up like that?'

'I been thinking a long time and I don't know nor can guess.'

'You said a lot of rotten meat came out which you had to bury.'

He looked up above my head and then down again.

'I've buried some sacks now and again for 'em. But then they do have a lot of meat from me, like. It *could* be they don't like it. It *could* be.'

'You know it isn't.'

'Not enough to do something definite,' he said. 'But now they done little Farney

like that I might get a bit more nosy. Yes.'
He nodded as if he had made up his
mind. 'Yes, I might.'

'You must be careful,' I said. 'You
buried sacks of meat you suspected was
human. The police wouldn't like that.'

'First off I never thought of it. I
thought it was meat I sold. It was only
after a while I began to think, 'How much
did I sell? Have they gone vegetarian?'
Then I started to worry.'

'Why didn't you do something then?'

He stared at the ground.

'Well, Farney was there, and I wasn't
sure about the Old Man. Not that he
wasn't dead, I mean.'

'But you had started to be unhappy
about it all?'

'Yes.'

'But what about when the Baroness
was alive?'

'There wasn't the people there then.
They didn't want so much, you see.
'Sides, the old woman arranged things
herself. She were in command. There
weren't any doubt what to do, when and
how. She was old but strong as an ox.'

'When did you last see the Old Man alive?'

'Nine month back. That was when Farney got worried.'

'Farne told you?'

'Yes.'

'But did you see the Old Man?'

'I've never seen him. He was a hermit. Didn't show himself. Farney saw him now and then, but not much then.'

'So if he'd died years ago you wouldn't know?'

He stared.

'Come to think now — no. I suppose I wouldn't. Not for sure. But she died them three year back, because there was the funeral.'

'The Old Man didn't go to it?'

'He never went to anything. Hermits don't. There was a wreath of flowers. I 'member that.'

'Who did go, then?'

'Philips. There was just this ox-cart and Philips walking behind. It was like the way she'd lived. Stark.'

'Where was she buried?'

'There's a little chapel up through the

woods. Don't been used these many years, but all the Cardwells is up there. Two hundred years of 'em.'

He looked at me sharply.

'Shouldn't go there,' he said. 'If ever there was a place a man could believe in ghosts, that's it.'

'I'm not going there,' I said. 'I'm going back to the house.'

He shook his head.

'Why don't you jest go, then? I don't want to bury no more rotten meat.'

'I don't believe I'd get out. It's a narrow track right back to the road. The easiest place in the world to stage a car wreck.'

He shrugged.

'I hope you've luck,' he said.

'Thanks.' I went out and turned to the cart road.

'You going up there?' he said, and loaded his gun. 'I'll cover for you, but you'll be alone at the top, boy.'

'Thanks again.'

I knew he was doing it for Farne, but it was a very useful contribution to my journey.

Provided, of course, that he hadn't been putting on a grief act. But I felt he couldn't be so good an actor as to have been able to keep it up so long under my very suspicious eye.

To show him my complete understanding of the situation, I also let him see my Smith & Wesson as I took it out of my pocket and slipped off the safety catch. He nodded slightly.

He watched me as I started off up the cobbled track to the woods above. The moon was bright, and but for the sound of the distant water on the rocks, everything was still.

I did not think then that anyone was waiting for me in the woods. I thought that when they suspected I had got clear and was loose in the grounds, they would get back to the house and wait.

For if I found anything in the woods that incriminated them I would go back there, either to get my car or to try and find Cardwell.

Whatever happened, Cardwell was the key to this mystery, whether he was alive or dead. And if Mrs. Grobe was right and

Daffyd wrong, Cardwell might have been the inmate of the coffin at the solitary funeral while his wife still commanded the house.

Strangely enough, the employment of a staff of women was not so strange if a woman alone was the employer, or a man alone. When it was unlikely was if the husband and wife were still alive together, taking into account their reputed characters.

Reputed characters. There was the weakness. The characters might have been built up like fiction by the present staff, for that would be an easy job; so little was known of the shy pair.

The woods were quiet when I reached the top of the slope. I went off the track and in amongst the trees, then stopped to look around me.

Nothing moved. Even the rabbits seemed to be waiting.

I went on until, beyond the edge of the trees, I could see the overgrown shape of the house standing against the sky. I stopped again then and looked carefully all round me.

Nothing was to be seen moving, but I had an instinctive feeling that somebody was hiding near me.

The trees made a twisted maze of shapes and shadows which could have hidden a person as I hoped they hid me. The move in such a case is not to make one and stand quite still. I did that and waited. When I began to feel I could stand like that no longer there was a movement near me.

It was no more than a small rustle of leaves as a foot moved but in that stillness it was enough to get a fair direction.

'Stay where you are,' I said quietly, but loud enough to carry. 'I have a gun on you.'

I heard a muttered oath of old English origin.

'All right, Johnnie. It's me.'

The woman's voice was instantly recognisable.

'Step out slowly, Laura. You know the rules.'

She stepped out slowly, knowing the rules, for she had her hands on top of her head.

'Surely you can trust me,' she said.

'Why? Give me a reason I can agree with.'

I went to her and patted the places where she might have a weapon, but she had nothing. I gestured and she dropped her hands.

'I came to find you, you nuthead,' she said quietly.

'Snap. I was just going to look for you.' I smiled at her and she smiled back, and I kept my revolver close to my heart.

'I had to make a decision,' she said, 'as to who was likely to kill me first, so I came to find you.'

'It's a backhanded calculation you offer,' I said. 'What do you want to give away?'

'The set-up — if you're going to guarantee me a ride home.'

'In what? A hearse? Think it out first, Laura. I can't guarantee myself, let alone you. If you tell me what's going on, how do I know it isn't a ready-made noose?'

'All right. Ask me. Then you'll only hear what you want to know. I can't cheat then, can I?'

'You could cheat anyway, but just for a start: Is the Old Man alive?'

'I think he is.'

'You think he is? After three years living in that house, you think he is?'

'I've never seen the old sod, if you must know, and I haven't heard him speak, but that's part of his game. It frightens more if he's always unseen.'

'But why does it frighten you?'

'Because, dear Johnnie, if we don't do as we're told we get died off.'

'But Laura, you go into town to see that lawyer. Now if you can do that, you can bolt and not be afeard of being died off.'

'I never go alone. Nobody ever gets out of here alone.'

'Then who goes with you?'

'I don't know. My dear man, if we did know, would we be so frightened?'

'I saw you walking back from going there. You were alone.'

'Once we're in the grounds — yes. But not alone to get out.'

'I see. Then why do you want me to guarantee something you know I couldn't do because we'd be picked up before we'd got out?'

'Because you're a good shot, and you know the business of getting out. I don't. I just know how to get in.'

'Come off it, Laura. You say you don't go alone. Who goes with you? You don't know. So how do they go with you?'

'There's a Land Rover here in the big barn. If we go, that goes behind. It follows. It waits with you. You try and lose it and there it is ahead of you. It's a demonstration of absolute power, like the woodworm hunts. You do it because if you don't you know what the answer is — in the back of the neck. We've seen so many murders here that it has a — what do you say? — a salutary effect on our morale. So we behave and do our Pavlov acts and we wait.'

'To inherit?'

'Of course. Once you get into this sort of thing and there is a strict promise that can't be broken, it's a tie all round.'

'How can you be sure you'll get it?'

'I go into the solicitor's every so often to make sure that nothing can be altered in the will now. It's tied up, Johnny. We made no mistake about that. If anything, the mistake we did make was in expecting the old man to die much sooner than this.'

'Couldn't you have made it sooner?'

'I've told you — I've seen too many murders to try it. Besides, how do you murder someone you never see? It would take very careful doing anyhow, because the will states that if he dies from unnatural causes, all bequests are automatically revoked. Well, I mean, you'd expect that, wouldn't you?'

'How many murders have you seen there?'

'I haven't actually seen them, but I know they happened. These men come and they disappear. It's really a human disposal unit.'

'What men?'

'Traitors, terrorists, spies. Anyone he finds is working against the country. He's positively lunatic. I believe his wife was worse, jackboots and all.'

'You don't think she's still alive and he's dead?'

She stood very still for a second or more.

'Why did you ask that?'

'The idea occurred. After all, if you never see the operator, how can you be sure who he is?'

'Of course. That is a point, but she died before we came and I've never seen any trace of a woman running the house. You can tell the difference in the management.'

'I suppose you can. Now when I came you all gave me the impression you met him for dinner every night, that he called you in, mauled you about and generally gave the impression of being very much alive. That was all fabrication?'

'That was the standard story for a visitor, to make him at ease by making things seem natural. To tell the truth wouldn't have seemed natural, would it? An invisible lunatic doing Pavlov tricks with gongs and klaxons has got something bizarre about it, even vicious.

'With the picture of an old man having got to a bottom-patting second boyhood making sudden noises to frighten people

216

it was understandable.'

'And what about the dinners that never come?'

'But they do come — in the end. There was a mess up tonight — '

'Because the cook was murdered,' I said.

Again Laura went quiet for a short while.

'Oh. She was? I expected it but didn't know it had happened already. She sort of ran out of guile in the kitchen. Started yelling about having had enough of it. What she meant was she'd had enough of spying for the police.

'She went on and explained that, hoping it would put her on our side. But Philips and Trellis, well, they started an inquisition and once they begin you might as well cough up the lot — I'm sorry about her. But when someone collapses like that and tries to change sides — well, you can't trust them, either, can you?'

I looked towards the house, still and silent in the moonlight.

'The woman said he lived in a room

with no doors,' I said. 'Do you know where that is?'

Laura cocked her head.

'She said that? What woman?'

'Mrs. Grobe. She also said she had seen the baroness three months ago.'

'For certain?'

'She said so. It seemed that the Baroness wanted something of her son's, and the son took it to the house and hasn't been seen since.'

'Three months ago? I don't remember anything special then. But she must be dead. If they were both alive, Cardwell and his wife, we should hear them talk or something. Besides, they would both eat.'

'I wanted to ask you, what food does go to the invisible man?'

'Oh, food does go. Philips takes that. Nobody else and nobody goes with him. I've never seen food for two go.'

'Farne was very fond of Cardwell, wasn't he?'

'Farne was simple. I think he felt that Cardwell owned his life, you know, like a grateful dog.'

'Then he must have seen the old man?'

'Well, a long time ago. I suppose when she was alive.'

'Farne's dead.'

Again she seemed startled. I told her how it had happened. Then I told her I had recognised the man on the identity sheet I had found.

'Then the trap was meant for you, ducky,' she said, 'not for him. There could have been files down there. Files of dead men wouldn't have been left lying around the secretary's office, in case anybody really nosy — like you — got in.'

'Who is the old man in the woods here?'

'I don't know. He's like one of the trees — he just belongs.'

'He thinks you're a lot of lunatics.'

'And we think he's a lunatic, so what? Look, take me out of here. Time's getting short.'

'Before what?'

'Before I'm found missing. Then they'll look. You see, Mrs. Fox got a sniff of the fact I knew you. Maybe it was only a suspicion, but when I'm missing, she'll be sure.

'And it's in your own interest to try and get out now, Johnny. You're for the chop, so what's the risk of trying a dive?'

'Curiosity. I want to find the old man in that house.'

'Now? I've been trying three years! How could you be so clever?'

'You didn't know about the room with no doors.'

'And where will you look for that? There's no such place I ever saw.'

'There is a steam organ.'

'For heaven's sake, what's that got to do with anything? It was the alarm thing that made all the row.'

'Then you had to march about and make more row.'

'I've explained all that! Don't waste more time. Try and beat it out now.'

'I want to know, who keeps the boiler going all the time for that organ?'

'Philips does it himself. The old man's crazy about hot water. It's an oil fired boiler. Philips watches it. Now let's — '

'You stay in the woods,' I said. 'If you see Daffyd, don't worry too much. He's changed sides.'

'No, don't — ' She gave up. I heard her swear, then I went on towards the side of the house, keeping to the fringe of the wood.

My aim was the back of the house and the baroness's Quiet Way In.

★   ★   ★

I had no illusions about not being expected. I had been chased through the wood and left below because of the booby trap, but I was sure the unexpected result of its operation would be known by then. Daffyd could not just retire and await his execution squad. He would have to keep up the pretence that he was still reliable while he thought what he would do later, when opportunity occurred.

Until then he would be, though not actively against me, certainly not with me.

The trees still covered me when I came round within sight of the house back. The kitchen door was wide open and yellow light came out, but I saw nobody moving about inside.

The journey to the back garden meant

twenty yards of open ground, so I ran it fast, the revolver in my right hand and my eyes right, trying to catch any slight movement at the house back. I saw nothing move at all.

I had seen the house from this angle before, but with the upholstery of the overwhelming ivy it was difficult to make out exactly what shape it really was. I estimated there was room for attics at the back but there were no windows up there.

With some care for silence and alert for any movement at the house, I made my way down the garden to the part of the wall the woman had described.

With the ivy covering the wall there was no sign of any opening so I had to take the risk of using cook's torch very briefly. The second or two I held the light on and moved it across the surface of the ivy were tense, but suddenly I saw a vertical break in the twisted pattern of the climber's limbs and snapped the light off.

For a moment or two I waited, expecting to hear an alarm because the light had been spotted, but nothing came.

I fumbled in amongst the ivy. It was

quite a simple device; you just gripped the vine, pulled, and a section of the wall opened outwards, not very far, but enough for one to slip in.

As a precaution I looked quickly round the garden but saw no one. I went into the opening and pulled the door shut behind me. Then I shone the torch again up a flight of very narrow rough wooden stairs to a blank-looking door at the top.

I went up and listened at the door. Hearing nothing, I pulled the door open and stepped into the cupboard where Mrs. Grobe had gone. Again I listened before stepping out into the empty room.

My mind was still set on the scene of the cook, hastily clutching a dressing gown round her and running to the door opposite hers across the passage.

When I set out into the corridor, everything was quiet but candlelight still shone down in the hall throwing up the railing pattern like stripes across the ceiling ahead of me.

I went very carefully, my pistol ready in my right hand, but the whole house seemed deserted. I began to wonder if the hunters were still out in the woods, but remembered Laura would not have gone that way if they were.

At the landing I stopped and looked down into the hall, but it was quiet and no movement disturbed the candle flame. As I crossed the open side to the other part of the corridor I wondered if the alarm gongs and bug hunts were enjoyed only when a doomed visitor was in the house.

I came to the door opposite cook's and stopped. I looked from one door to the other, then went and opened the cook's.

The room was tidy. The body had gone, doubtless to be disposed of like all the others which I believed had passed through that place.

There was still no sound as I closed the door and turned to the opposite one. I crossed to it and listened. There was a very faint, but steady hissing from somewhere. I thought of the steam organ in the attic.

With my hand on the door handle I had the feeling somebody was watching me. I looked left, down to my bedroom.

Someone was standing in the doorway looking towards me.

I looked to the right. A woman was standing at the top of the stairs looking at me. She was silhouetted against the dull candlelight below so that I could not tell who she was.

Neither moved. I was fairly trapped there, but it was not unexpected.

In that moment I decided it would be better to fight the Big Boss than argue with the assistants.

I turned the handle, opened the door and stepped into the room.

The light was bright in there. It was provided by a hissing Tilley lamp which burnt in the middle of the room with no doors!

The ceiling of the room was on the floor with a shining pillar in each corner standing up to where the ceiling had been. On the platform was a desk, a table, a chair and a man sitting in it.

The man did not move. He looked like a skeleton which had settled on its joints and which, if moved, would collapse into a heap of bones spilling on to the floor.

The four pillars around him were steam rams which carried the contraption up or set it down again. Through the hole above I could see part of a steam organ from an old fairground roundabout.

He spoke. It sounded like a death rattle in his bony throat.

'They were all — traitors,' he said.

He seemed unable to lift his head to look at me, but with a bony claw, he grasped a bulb on the end of a tube which looped up and disappeared somewhere into the machinery in the darkness above.

Then it started. The row was indescribable. The drums, the gongs, the tambourines, the howling rasp of the Klaxon, the hiss of steam, and then with a louder hissing that the steam organ was clearly intended to drown, the whole 'room' was lifted from the ground.

I saw him drop the bulb, and then I saw him die. He tried to lift his head, failed, choked, then collapsed into an unmistakeable death fall from the chair.

Slowly the room rose up into the ceiling and then the noise stopped and there was a sudden awful silence.

As I stood there, I expected the din of the bug hunters to start outside, but it did not come. After the brightness of the Tilley lamp, now gone to the ceiling, it was very dark.

I opened the door. Nobody moved out there. I was ready to shoot if anyone tried to get near me, but as I opened the door wider I saw two women standing only a few feet away, faintly lit by the candles from down in the hall.

They did not move, but Mrs. Fox near the stairs, took a deep breath as if to ask a question, but she did not. Miss Lewson who had come up from my bedroom stood very still, watching me, but making no move towards me.

Then I saw the housekeeper, Trellis appear silently at the top of the stairs. She stopped dead, looking towards me.

With some surprise I realised the three women were waiting for me to do something.

I said, 'He's dead.'

The secretary took a sharp breath.

'Did you kill him?' she hissed.

'No. He just came to the end of a

natural life. He'd lived quite long enough, surely.'

Mrs. Fox sighed with relief. On the stairs the housekeeper relaxed visibly. They had feared a violent death, but there had not been one.

The secretary was first to grasp the full importance of the situation.

'Get Philips,' she said sharply.

They left me to look for the butler, but they didn't find him. Philips must have got wind of what had happened, for by the time they went to shut him up — or down, probably both — he had vanished.

I went along and got my things from the bedroom. From that time on the affairs of that house were the police business. I had found out everything I had been sent to find and that was the end of that.

When I got downstairs the farmer was at the open doorway. He looked askance at me.

'The Old Man's dead,' I said.

'Thank the lord for that,' he said. He breathed deep. 'Cor, it's like being let out of prison.' He looked round at the night.

'Where're the women? They'll go, you know. They'll go to wait for their money. They were all promised money, you know, to do as they were told. Not that they did any killing. They made the bed for it, you might say, but Philips was the butcher.

'I think he killed Farney because he thought he was getting near to telling you what was going on. I think you rattled that butler.'

'I'm glad I rattled somebody.'

'Oh, there's some rattlin' to come yet,' he said. 'Those beautiful ladies, now. They all think they're going to get fortunes, because there's no relative. It all depends on that — being no relative.'

He laughed quite heartily then.

'The old man of the woods?' I said.

'You guessed,' he said.

'I saw him sleeping in a chair in the study.'

'Yes, he used to come in when he knew the women weren't about. It made him laugh, he said.'

'Who is he?'

'He's old Cardwell's brother. Born in

Australia, but families get broke up accidentally and in other ways, so he didn't turn up for so many years, but then he did.

'Now, he don't want much, Alan. He loves nature and animals but he didn't love his brother for being greedy, and got fun out of being a nuisance by just being about, but nobody knowing quite where and that.

'You know, master,' he said, looking at me frankly, 'I sometimes reckon that Alan was the reason old Cardwell come to be a hermit. I mean, after all, there's got to be a reason, han't there, even for barmies?'

'Once a man's dead you can't be sure of any of his reasons.'

'Well, taken one way or another, reasons is mostly fear.'

THE END

DEATH IN RETREAT

George Douglas

On a day of retreat for clergy at Overdale House, a resident guest, Martin Pender, is foully murdered. The primary task of the Regional Homicide Squad is to track down the bogus parson who joined the retreat. Subsequent events show that serious political motives lie behind the killing, but the basic lead to it all is missing. Then, three young tearaways corner the killer in the woods, and a chess problem, set out on a board, yields vital evidence.

THE CALIGARI COMPLEX

Basil Copper

Mike Faraday, the laconic L.A. private investigator, is called in when macabre happenings threaten the Martin-Hannaway Corporation. Fires, accidents and sudden death are involved; one of the partners, James Hannaway, inexplicably fell off a monster crane. Mike is soon entangled in a web of murder, treachery and deceit and through it all a sinister figure flits; something out of a nightmare. Who is hiding beneath the mask of Cesare, the somnambulist? Mike has a tough time finding out.

MIX ME A MURDER

Leo Grex

A drugged girl, a crook with a secret, a
doctor with a dubious past, and
murder during a shooting affray
— described as a 'duel' by the Press
— become part of a developing
mystery in which a concealed denoue-
ment is unravelled only when the last
danger threatens. Even then, the
drama becomes a race against time
and death when Detective Chief
Superintendent Gary Bull insists on
playing his key role of hostage to
danger.